WE THINK YOU'LL LOVE THIS BOOK

It's got a Mark *and* a Shark . . .

It's got an enormous polar bear *and* a rather small penguin . . .

It's got a brave Darcy *and* a magnificent horse called Clive . . .

It's got a gang of really bad baddies *and* some very unusual office furniture . . .

AND it's got lots and lots of ice cream!
(and absolutely NO seals)

JOHN DOUGHERTY   pictures by KATIE ABEY

MARK AND SHARK

DETECTIVING AND STUFF

OXFORD
UNIVERSITY PRESS

OXFORD
UNIVERSITY PRESS

Great Clarendon Street, Oxford OX2 6DP

Oxford University Press is a department of the University of Oxford.
It furthers the University's objective of excellence in research, scholarship,
and education by publishing worldwide. Oxford is a registered trade mark of
Oxford University Press in the UK and in certain other countries

First published 2019

Database right Oxford University Press (maker)

British Library Cataloguing in Publication Data
Data available

ISBN: 978-0-19-276898-8

1 3 5 7 9 10 8 6 4 2

Printed in Great Britain

Paper used in the production of this book is a natural,
recyclable product made from wood grown in sustainable forests.
The manufacturing process conforms to the environmental
regulations of the country of origin.

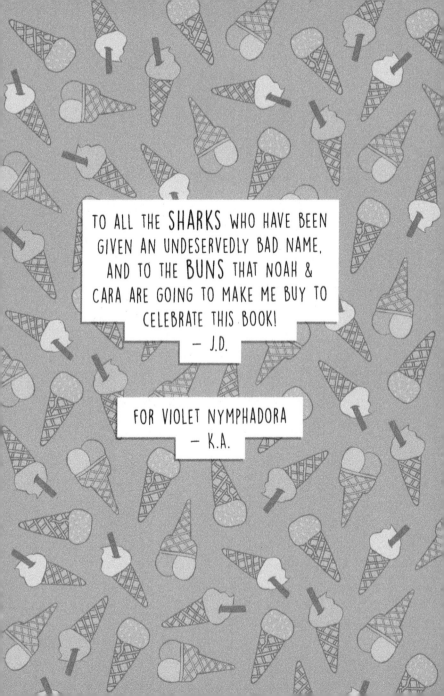

TO ALL THE **SHARKS** WHO HAVE BEEN
GIVEN AN UNDESERVEDLY BAD NAME,
AND TO THE **BUNS** THAT NOAH &
CARA ARE GOING TO MAKE ME BUY TO
CELEBRATE THIS BOOK!
— J.D.

FOR VIOLET NYMPHADORA
— K.A.

CHAPTER ONE

That day, like so many days, began with a shark BURSTING through the door.

'SEAL!' the shark yelled, and jumped at me, sharp teeth flashing in the morning light like tiny white pixie hats of death.

If I'd been a less quick-thinking sort of Mark, this story would have ended right there, with little bits of Mark all over the office, and a shark standing on the welcome mat chewing and saying, 'This seal tastes a bit funny.'

But you don't get to my age in this city without knowing that the best way to repel a shark attack is to **biff** the shark on the nose. So I **biffed** the shark on the nose.

'OW!' yelled the shark, leaping backwards. 'What did you do that for?'

'You were trying to eat me,' I explained, with what I felt was admirable patience. 'Again.'

'Yeah, alright, I was,' admitted the shark cheerfully. 'But it's not my fault. I thought you were a seal.'

'Yes, I know,' I said. 'But I'm not. Honestly, Shark, how long have we known each other? Surely by this time you ought to be able to tell the difference between me and a seal.'

Shark shrugged. 'I wouldn't keep mistaking you for a seal if you didn't keep dressing like one.'

'I'm not dressed anything like a seal!' I said.

This was true. Anyone who's ever met Shark takes particular care to not dress like a seal. Sadly, it rarely makes any difference.

'Oh,' Shark said. 'OK. But I was definitely

expecting to find a seal in here.'

This was a new one. Taking Shark gently by the fin, I led her out into the hallway and pointed at the shiny brass plaque fastened to the wall just outside the office.

'Read the top line,' I told her.

Squinting, she read, 'Mark and Shark . . .'

'Right,' I said. 'So what would you expect to find in there?'

She rubbed her nose thoughtfully. 'Um . . . a Mark and a Shark, I suppose.'

'Does it say anything about seals?' I asked.

'Nope.'

'Right,' I said. 'No seals. Just a Mark and a Shark.'

She peered through the doorway. 'Wait a minute,' she said. 'It's clearly some kind of trick. There aren't any Marks or Sharks in there.'

'That,' I said, 'is because we're standing

out here.'

She looked at me, and then checked her reflection in the brass plaque. 'Oh, yeah,' she said. 'What are we doing out here instead of in there?'

'I . . . never mind,' I said, and went back inside. Shark HOPPED in behind me, shutting the door after her.

Seconds later, she yelled, 'SEAL!' and JUMPED on Shadwell, the office cat.

Shadwell **biffed** her on the nose.

'That's not a seal either, Shark,' I said, as Shark SQUEALED and LEAPT backwards. 'It's the cat.'

'OK,' said Shark, rubbing her nose with one pointy fin. 'What are we doing today?'

Being friends with a shark is never dull—though it's not as dangerous as you might think. Lots of things are more likely to kill you than a shark—lightning; baths; even toasters. Look it up; you'll see I'm right.

Mind you, even in a city as BIG and WILD and CRAZY as this one, there are people who say kids and sharks shouldn't be friends. They don't usually say it to me, though—mostly because, if they do, I point at them and shout, 'SEAL!' and then they have to spend the next few minutes **biffing** Shark on the nose before I set her straight. Shark's my best friend, however different we might be, and that's all there is to it. That's why, when I decided to set up a detective agency, I asked her to join me.

Shark wasn't keen. 'I'm no good at detectiving,' she said.

'What are you good at?' I asked.

Shark shrugged. 'Stuff,' she said.

So we went looking for an office, and when we found this one, we put up a brass plaque that says:

MARK & SHARK
DETECTIVING AND STUFF

Just call on us if you've got any detecting
that needs doing. Or stuff, for that matter.
But particularly detecting, because we don't
get asked to do enough of that. OK, so far we
haven't been asked to do any. But it'll happen;
just you wait.

Which, getting back to that particular
morning, was what Shark and I were about
to do: wait. But first we had to get the office
ready. I grabbed a broom and gave the floor a
quick once-over, and then I went down to the
door at the other end of the room and turned
the handle.

Immediately there was a SCUFFLING and
THUMPING from the other side of the door, as
if a pack of excitable wooden Labradors was

trying to get out. I put my shoulder to the door and heaved it open, and out scampered about half a dozen office desks.

'Down! Get down!' I said, as they PUSHED and JOSTLED to get close to me. 'Get down, Chip! Down, Hardwood! Good desks! Get down!'

Of course, they didn't get down. They just kept LEAPING and BOUNDING and YELPING, until I took a nameplate from my pocket. It said:

MARK
HEAD OF DETECTIVING

'Now,' I said, 'Who wants to be my desk today?'

Immediately, the desks froze in position, TREMBLING with

excitement. I made a bit of a show of choosing one, and then plonked the nameplate down on Knots, a desk I hadn't used for a few days. She YELPED elatedly and SCURRIED off to stand proudly near the door.

'And who wants to be Shark's desk?' I went on, producing a nameplate that read:

SHARK
HEAD OF STUFF

There was considerably less enthusiasm this time, and a couple of desks shuffled quietly back into the storeroom, but eventually Chunky clumped reluctantly forward. I set down the nameplate, grabbed a couple of chairs, and lifted our old computer onto my desk.

And just then, I heard the building's outer door open.

CHAPTER TWO

'Customer!' I hissed, and we rushed to our desks, where I tried to look busy by typing frantically on the computer, while Shark tried to look busy by sticking her head in a wastepaper basket.

The office door opened, to reveal a large rectangular block of white fur that completely filled the frame. It RIPPLED as it SQUEEZED through the doorway, almost flowing into the room, where it straightened up and revealed itself to be a huge, fierce-looking polar bear. She shook out her fur, put on the pork pie hat she held in one paw, and lumbered menacingly over to me.

Knots shifted uneasily, and I gave her a reassuring polish with my sleeve. 'Easy! Good desk,' I murmured. Then I turned my attention to what I very much hoped was a customer with a case for us, and not a wild animal with an unusual liking for hats and a taste for detective kebabs.

'Hello!' I said, as cheerfully and hopefully as I could manage. 'Welcome to Mark and Shark, Detectiving and Stuff. Which department would you like?'

'Stuff,' said the polar bear curtly.

'Certainly,' I said, filled with—in equal parts—disappointment that I wasn't, at last, going to get a proper mystery to solve; and relief that I wasn't going to be eaten by a polar bear. 'You'll need to speak to Shark, our Head of Stuff.' My old swivel chair SQUEAKED loudly as I turned and called, 'Shark! Customer! *Not a seal*, OK?'

'Oh,' said Shark, who had been about to leap. 'OK. Good morning sir or madam, how can I help you today?' she continued, reading from a big sheet of paper where I'd written, in very large letters, instructions for greeting a customer.

The polar bear, clearly unimpressed, looked at Shark. 'Why have you got that funny metal veil on your head?'

'It's not a veil,' said Shark, slightly scornfully. 'It's a wastepaper basket.'

The bear stared at her, unblinkingly. 'Then why,' she asked again, 'have you got it on your head?'

'It's just something she does,' I told the bear. '*But not normally in front of the customers,*' I added in a hinting sort of voice.

'Oh,' said Shark, taking the hint. 'Right. Yes. Sorry.' With a sudden twitch of her head she shook the wastepaper basket off, making Chunky JUMP with alarm. The wastepaper basket bounced across the floor, rolled to a stop, picked itself up and shuffled embarrassedly back to its place. 'Now,' Shark continued, reading off the sheet again, 'what sort of Stuff can we help you with?'

The polar bear leaned over her, front paws on Chunky, who let out a little frightened whimper and tried to shuffle backwards, but found himself unable to move.

'Business stuff,' she rumbled.

'OK,' said Shark.

I knew from experience that this was where I had to join in. Shark didn't really have the hang of asking questions to find out what the customer wanted, and if the silence went on too long she was likely to forget there was a customer in the room at all and start leaping on things.

'What sort of business stuff?' I asked.

Turning to me with predatory speed, the bear leaned in alarmingly close. Her breath was kind of fishy.

'I want you,' she said, 'to sell ice cream.'

'OK,' said Shark. Then she scratched her head with one fin. 'Wait a minute. We haven't got any ice cream.'

'No,' said the bear impatiently, 'but I have.'

'OK,' said Shark. 'So why do you want more ice cream?'

'I don't!' said the bear. 'I've got lots of ice cream. What I haven't got is someone to sell ice cream.'

'OK,' said Shark. 'So ... who's going to sell the ice cream?'

The bear stared. 'Well ... you!' she said.

'OK,' said Shark. She paused, and scratched her head again. 'But ... we haven't got any ice cream.'

Now the bear glared. 'But I have!'

'Then why do you need some more?'

'I don't need some more!' she roared. 'I've got lots of ice cream! I want you to sell it!'

'OK,' said Shark, pretending to take notes. 'Have you thought of just eating it?'

This seemed like a good moment for me to join in the conversation again. 'Shark,' I said, 'I think what's going on here is that our client, here, runs an ice-cream business. She wants us to work for her and sell her ice cream to other people, and then give her the money.'

The bear straightened up, towering over me. I felt suddenly small, dwarfed by her great bulk. Her eyes, small dark buttons set in the snowy landscape of her fur, bored into mine. Slowly, exasperatedly, she shook her great white head.

'Smart work, kid,' she growled. 'Ever thought of being a detective?' She sighed heavily, blowing her fishy breath right in my face. 'You going to take the job, or not?'

I shrugged, deciding to ignore the sarcasm. It'd be nice to get out of the office, even if we weren't going to do any detecting.

'Sure,' I said. 'Lead on, um . . . What do we

call you, anyhow?'

'Ursula,' growled the bear, taking her hat off again and SQUEEZING herself through the office door. I shrugged once more, and followed, Shark HOPPING happily behind me.

'So,' I asked, as we headed along the hallway, 'how come you suddenly need new ice-cream sellers?'

Ursula paused, fixing me with those dark buttons. 'My last seller quit this morning. Suddenly. Said she'd had a better offer, and she was fed up with driving my scrappy old van.'

She flung open the building's outer door, and my jaw dropped. Because the ice-cream van parked outside the office building was the most ASTONISHING piece of machinery I had ever seen in my whole life. It GLEAMED. It SHONE. It SPARKLED like the sparkliest sparkler that ever sparkled. Its paintwork curled and flowed in elegant whorls of pale cream and rich deep reds, tempting you closer. From bumper to bumper, it was sheer shiny perfection.

'Scrappy old van?' I breathed. 'But . . . it's BEAUTIFUL!'

The bear looked at me as if I'd lost it. Then she turned and looked, and *she* lost it. With an EARSPLITTING roar, she dropped onto all fours and hurled herself at the van.

CHAPTER THREE

I don't mind telling you, I had no idea what was happening. One moment this crazy bear was asking me and Shark to drive her ice-cream van, and the next she looked like she was all set to knock it over.

She didn't knock it over. Instead, with a bellow of 'PILBEAM!' she LEAPT head first into the serving hatch.

'What's a pilbeam?' Shark asked. Her question was answered just a moment later, as the passenger door of the van BURST open and out jumped a penguin.

'SEAL!' yelled Shark, and LEAPT on the
penguin.

'EEEK!' squeaked the penguin.

'HEY!' shouted a tall, thin girl, leaping out
after the penguin and biffing Shark on the nose.

'OW!' yelped Shark, dropping the penguin.
'What did you do that for?'

'You were trying to eat Mr Pilbeam!' the girl shouted.

'ROOOAAAAARRRR!'

roared Ursula, who appeared to have got stuck in the hatch.

'I'll sue!' shrieked the penguin, trembling and trying to hide under the van.

'He's a seal!' protested Shark. 'You're supposed to eat seals!'

'He's as much of a seal as I am, you idiot!' shouted the girl.

'SEAL!' yelled Shark, and jumped on the girl. 'Ow!' she added, as the girl **biffed** her on the nose again. 'What did you do that for?'

'You were trying to eat me!' the girl shouted.

'But you said you were a seal!' Shark complained.

'No, I didn't!'

'Yes, you did! You said you were as much of a seal as that seal!' Shark insisted. 'And that seal is a seal! So if you're as much of a seal as that seal is, you're a seal!'

'He's a penguin, tunabrain!'

'ROOOAAAAARRRR!!!!'

roared Ursula, still trying to squeeze her enormous rear through the serving hatch.

The girl glared at Shark, and then reached under the van, pulled the penguin out and began to brush him down. 'It's OK, Mr Pilbeam,' she said. 'You're safe now.'

The penguin—Pilbeam—looked daggers at Shark. 'You ought to be in prison, you fishy freak. Or an aquarium, anyway.'

'OK,' said Shark cheerfully.

Ursula appeared to be calming down. She'd stopped roaring, and was no longer WRIGGLING her hind-portions in a vain attempt to get into the van. In fact, judging by the faint GRUNTING sounds and the way her legs were sticking out behind her, she was trying to go into reverse; and she appeared to be succeeding, albeit incredibly slowly. It was like watching someone trying to squeeze the last morsel of bizarrely furry toothpaste out of the biggest toothpaste tube in the world.

The girl turned to me. She was tall and gangly, knees dangling from her bright yellow dungaree shorts and elbows sticking awkwardly out of the sleeves of a red T-shirt. Her hair was done up in neat, tight cornrows, with one slim plait hanging down at the back, and her eyes were bright and confident.

'And you!' she said angrily. 'Can't you keep your friend here under control? Don't you know how dangerous sharks are?'

'They're not that dangerous!' I protested. 'More people are killed by TOASTERS every year than sharks!'

'Oh, yeah?' she retorted. 'I've never had a toaster try to eat me!'

'Well, just wait till one mistakes you for a piece of bread,' I said. Not the wittiest of comebacks, so I quickly followed up with, 'Anyway, what were you two doing in our client's van?'

Pilbeam let out a scornful, honking laugh, right in my face—or as close to it as he could get, being about half my height.

'Ha hahaha ha hONK! Ha ha ha ha ha ha ha HONNNNK!!! HONK HONK ha ha ha HONK HONK OWFFFFF mmmm mmmm mmmm mmmm!'

It's infuriating to have a penguin laughing right in your face. But if a penguin is laughing in your face, it's so sweetly satisfying when a polar bear suddenly lands, bottom-first, right on top of it.

'Mmmmmf!' Pilbeam continued, from somewhere underneath Ursula's expansive rear end. 'Mmmmf! Mmmmmmmmf!'

A flipper poked weakly out from under Ursula's thigh. The girl grabbed it and pulled; with a POP Pilbeam emerged, looking shaken and tousled. Once more the girl helped him to his feet and brushed him down. Pilbeam glared at Ursula and straightened his slightly crumpled beak.

'I assume that by "client" you mean this . . . bear,' he said coldly. 'And I'll thank you to keep her out of my ice-cream van!'

It was my turn to look puzzled. 'Your van?'

'My van,' said Pilbeam. 'You didn't think it belonged to the bear, did you?

Ha ha ha HONNNK . . . !'

The laugh was cut short as Ursula rose to her feet with a roar. Pilbeam squeaked and dodged; suddenly he was cowering behind the girl's legs, using her as a human shield. Ursula reared up, her muzzle wrinkling in a wild and savage snarl, clawed paw raised as if to strike.

The girl stood tall, too, though nowhere near as tall as Ursula. 'Oh, roar to you too,' she said. 'Pick on someone your own size, why don't you.'

She was so thin that if Ursula had hit out at her, the wind from the blow would have knocked her flat before the paw ever reached her. Despite that, she didn't seem scared at all.

'I don't know if you're waving hello at me with that paw,' the girl went on, 'but one thing I know is that you are not going to hit me with it. Not unless you want to spend the rest of your life in jail. Put it down.'

Ursula's black lips drew back, revealing her pale yellow teeth. She took a step forward.

The girl didn't move.

CHAPTER FOUR

The air CRACKLED with tension, and the threat of violence.

The girl folded her arms defiantly. Tall as she was, she looked tiny next to the bear; tiny and frail. If those claws came down on her head, she didn't stand a chance.

Then, slowly and reluctantly, Ursula lowered her paw.

'Now,' said the girl, 'what do you think you're doing, leaping into Mr Pilbeam's van like that and scaring the life out of both of us?'

'I wasn't scared!' protested Pilbeam, from behind the girl's legs.

'I got angry,' Ursula growled softly.

'Pilbeam's trying to ruin me.'

'How do you figure that out?' I asked.

'This is my territory!' she snapped. 'We made a deal: I sell ice cream round here; Pilbeam sells in the Harbourside District. But for years I've had my suspicions that he ain't sticking to his side of things—sneaking in to my territory to sell on a street here, an avenue there; eating into my profits month by month so that he gets richer as I get poorer. And now, suddenly, everywhere I go, Pilbeam's been there first in his shiny new van, selling everybody all the ice cream they can eat. I haven't sold a single cone in three days!'

'Don't blame me for your own failings, bear!' Pilbeam SQUAWKED, scurrying forward angrily. 'Eeep!' he added, scurrying back again at the sight of Ursula's FURIOUS scowl.

'And if that wasn't enough, this morning he steals my assistant!'

'Hey!' said the girl. 'Don't talk about me like I'm property! Nobody stole me! I got a new job with someone else, because you haven't paid me for weeks!'

Ursula seemed to shrink just a little. 'Business has been bad lately,' she said. 'You know that, Darcy. I'll pay you as soon as I can . . .'

'Mr Pilbeam's paying me now,' Darcy said. She shook her head sadly. 'I'm sorry, Ursula, but I need the money. I can't afford to wait.'

'OK, kid,' said Ursula brokenly. 'I get that you need a new job. But with Pilbeam? When he's driving me out of business?'

Pilbeam peeked out from behind the girl's legs again. 'You're driving yourself out of business, bear!' he squawked. 'That rattly old van of yours is a DISGRACE to the name of ice cream!' He began to back away, towards the passenger door of the van. 'Come on, Doris,' he ordered.

'My name's Darcy, Mr Pilbeam.'

The penguin waved a careless flipper. 'Whatever,' he said. 'Let's go. We've got ice cream to sell.'

As Pilbeam and Darcy climbed aboard the van, I looked from Pilbeam to Ursula, and back again. I wasn't sure which of them was the bad guy in this situation—maybe they both were. But in the last few minutes, Darcy had picked Pilbeam off the ground and brushed him down, twice; fought off a shark who was trying to eat him; and stood between him and an angry polar bear—and he hadn't once said, 'Thanks.' In fact, he couldn't even be bothered to remember her name. None of that, in my book, made him a good guy.

I suddenly realized something. 'Where's Shark?' I asked. I'd been so wrapped up with the whole Darcy-and-Pilbeam-versus-Ursula situation that I hadn't noticed her slipping off somewhere. 'Shark!' I called.

'Yes?' came her voice, and I looked to see her leaning out of the serving hatch of Pilbeam's van. A moment later, she added,

'WoOOoaaaaah!'

as somebody lifted her tail and tipped her out, head first, onto the pavement.

Darcy appeared behind her. 'And stay out!' she said, before she disappeared into the van again.

'What were you doing in Pilbeam's van?' I asked.

Shark looked up at me from the pavement. 'Ummm ... looking for clues,' she said.

'Clues about what? And—what's that white stuff on your nose?'

'It's not ice cream,' Shark said quickly. 'Definitely not vanilla. And there isn't any seal flavour; I've checked.'

With a smooth electric purr, Pilbeam and Darcy pulled away, revealing two things. One was that on the back of the van, painted in large letters, were the words, 'PILBEAM'S ICE CREAMS', which would have saved me a bit of trouble if I'd seen them earlier.

The other was that on the other side of the road stood the ugliest vehicle I had ever seen in my life. It was pretty much the exact opposite of Pilbeam's. It was BATTERED, and DENTED, and DIRTY. Patches of rust showed through the faded, flaking yellow paintwork. The driver's door was a dull grey and didn't quite fit the frame, and there was a small ragged-edged hole in the wing-panel beside it. At the front, between the headlights, a couple of wooden shafts had been fixed through the ancient radiator grille; and standing glumly between them was ...

'Is that a horse?' I asked.

Shark sat up. 'Oooh!' she said excitedly. 'Horsey!' She LEAPT to her tail and waved at the animal. 'Hello, horsey!'

The horse did not look impressed. Neither was I.

'Shark,' I said, 'what are you doing? You're meant to be a terrifying predator of the deep!'

'Well—yeah,' she agreed. 'But, look! It's a horsey!'

'Come on,' rumbled Ursula. 'Time for you two to do some work.'

We followed her across the road.

'So—wait,' I said. 'You've hired us to drive an ice-cream van that's so broken down it has to be pulled by a horse?'

Ursula glared at me. 'If you don't want the job, some other idiot'll take it.'

I shrugged. I'd rather have been detectiving, but work is work, and I always reckon it's better to take the job that's actually there than wait for the one that may never come.

Shark, by this time, was patting the horse on the nose, and making a proper fuss of it.

'Hello, horsey!' she was saying. 'Who's a lovely horsey? You are! What a good horsey! What's your name, horsey?'

The horse looked at her with gloom-filled eyes.

'Clive,' he said.

'OK,' said Shark. 'Shall we go for a clip-clop, horsey?'

Clive looked at her for what seemed like an age. Then he looked at me, and at Ursula, and back at Shark again.

'I suppose so,' he said dolefully. 'It's not as if I have anything better to do with my life than take a big dangerous fish with terrifyingly sharp teeth for a clip-clop.'

'Yay!' said Shark, bouncing up and down on tip-tail. 'Come on, Mark! The horsey's going to take us for a clip-clop!'

CHAPTER FIVE

Before the horsey could actually take us
for a clip-clop, Ursula had to give us our
instructions. Given the conversation which
had just taken place, I was kind of surprised
when she pulled out a map of the city and
drew a circle round the area we were standing
in.

'This,' she began, 'is my territory. It's
where I sell ice cream. So don't go beyond this
line . . .'

'Hang on,' I interrupted. 'Why should
we stick to the deal? Pilbeam's broken it; he's
selling on your patch.'

Ursula rounded on me, shoving her
muzzle in my face so close I could have

counted the individual hairs. 'Look, kid,' she GROWLED, hitting me with another blast of that fishy breath. 'I'm a polar bear, OK? I'm a territorial animal.'

'Sure,' I agreed. 'But if another predator invades your territory . . .'

'HAH!' she laughed, a great BARKING laugh so forceful I could actually smell different types of fish in it. There was definitely salmon, and, I thought, a hint of cod, too. 'Pilbeam? A predator? Don't make me laugh!'

'I'll try not to,' I coughed, trying to get the smell of fish out of my nostrils. 'But, look . . . Pilbeam's trying to run you out of business by selling to your customers, right?'

A deep growl rose in Ursula's throat. She nodded, though, which I took as encouragement to continue.

'And in that brand new electric van, he'll get round your territory far faster than Clive here's ever going to pull us. We'll be behind him all the way.'

We glanced at Clive, who—despite Shark's ongoing attempts to entertain him—didn't exactly look full of get-up-and-go. I'd never seen a horse who was less hot to trot.

'So what're you suggesting, kid?' Ursula snarled. 'We strike back? We go selling in Pilbeam's territory?'

'Nope,' I said. 'He'll have that covered, too.'

'Then what?' the bear almost roared.

'We go here,' I said, pointing to the map. 'The Inner West Side.'

Ursula's brow WRINKLED in puzzlement. 'Why there?'

I counted off on my fingers. 'One: it's not too far from here. I'm guessing Clive doesn't move so fast, especially when he's pulling a heavy vehicle, so we need to sell somewhere nearby.

'Two: It's in completely the opposite direction from the Harbourside District. If Pilbeam's trying to cover your territory and his, he won't have time to travel any further from home.

'And, three: let's face it, the Harbourside District is too classy for your van. It'd stick out like a sore paw. The Inner West Side, on the other hand . . .'

I let the sentence hang, but I could see Ursula finishing it off in her head. The Inner West Side was home to a few rough neighbourhoods. The sorts of places where people wouldn't be too proud to buy ice cream from a broken-down van pulled by the world's gloomiest horse.

'Yeah, OK,' she growled after a moment. 'Give it a go, kid.' She leaned in so close that her round black nose actually touched mine for a moment—it was surprisingly warm—and

drew her lips back again. Out of the corner
of my eye, I could see her long canine fangs.
They were disturbingly pointed—much like
her next comment. 'But do it properly. Don't
be too generous with the ice cream. Make sure
you get the right money from the customers.
Don't get the cones wet; that'll ruin them.
Oh—and remember: if anything goes wrong,
I'm holding you personally responsible.'

'OK,' I said. It came out as a hoarse
whisper; I cleared my throat and tried again.
'OK. Just one more thing . . .'

'WHAT?' she snarled impatiently.

'How much are you going to pay us? And when?'

Ursula's eyes narrowed, but I held her gaze. It was a fair question; Darcy had left because she wasn't being paid. I didn't want the same thing to happen to us.

'Tell you what, kid,' she said after a moment. 'I'll give you a share of whatever you make. And I'll pay you as soon as the round's over. How's that?'

I nodded. 'Come on, Shark. Let's get going!'

'Yay!' said Shark, scrambling into the van. 'Giddy-up, horsey!'

I scrambled in, too, and the horsey giddied up.

CHAPTER SIX

I hadn't been to the Inner West Side for a few months, and in that short time, it seemed to have got rougher. A LOT rougher. The place had got so run-down—graffiti; broken windows; grime and litter everywhere—that the van fitted right in. We CLIP—CLOPPED slowly through the streets, with the van's tinny and slightly out-of-tune chimes letting the customers know we were coming, and Clive giving us a running commentary of his woes all the way.

'It's no life for a horse,' he said, heaving a sigh. 'Pulling a van, I mean. It's too heavy. You

43

haven't got the brake on, have you?'

I checked. We hadn't.

'I miss Darcy,' Clive went on. 'Darcy was nice to me. And she didn't have big scary teeth. It's no fun without her around.'

'Don't worry about Shark's teeth,' I told him. 'She's not that scary, really.'

'Or dangerous,' Shark chipped in. 'I mean—I am dangerous, but I'm not as dangerous as a TOASTER.'

'I hate toasters,' Clive said gloomily.

It wasn't long before we saw a number of kids gathered by the roadside, clearly expecting us to stop. So we did.

'Quickly, Shark; grab a box of waffle cones,' I hissed, and went to stand at the serving hatch. 'Who's first?'

A little bright-eyed kid stepped forward, holding up a coin—but before she could even make her order, three figures appeared,

PUSHING their way through the crowd. All were hooded, masked, and dressed in black. I guessed that this was not a good sign.

The first—which looked like some kind of vacuum cleaner with a hose attachment—sucked the coin from the little girl's hand and SHOVED her roughly to one side. Another—which, going by its size and shape, could have been anything from a fat dog to a particularly fluffy sheep—BARGED the rest of the kids out of the way. The third reached up with three of its eight black-clad limbs and GRABBED hold of me. My best guess was that this one was a medium-sized octopus. It was either that, or eight snakes and a goldfish in a bowl.

'Gimme all the money,' she demanded.

'Kkkkkhhhhhhh,' I replied, suddenly unable to breathe.

'Hey!' the octopus said, squeezing a

little tighter. 'Who are you threatening, buster?'

Thankfully, the dog, or sheep, or whatever he was, noticed what was going on. 'He ain't threatening you, Tracy,' he said.

'Darn right he's threatening me!' said the octopus. 'He's turning darker! That's fighting talk where I'm from.'

'That's 'cos where you're from, everyone's an octopus,' explained the dog or sheep or whatever he was. 'People don't communicate by changing colour. You got hold of his breathing pipe, that's all.'

'You sure he ain't threatening me?'

'Positive. Only, let go of his breathing pipe, will ya?'

'Oh, OK,' said the octopus, and let go. Of my arms.

'Khhhh,' I said.

'No, dummy,' said the four-legged creature. 'The bit you're still holding. Let go of that bit.'

'Oh,' said the octopus, and let go of my throat, just in time. I SAGGED over the hatch, GASPING in lungfuls. She GRABBED me by the arm again. 'Now: gimme the money.'

'We haven't got any money,' I croaked, between gasps. 'This is our first stop. We haven't sold anything yet.'

'Oh,' said the octopus once more.

'Then give us all the ice cream,' said the vacuum cleaner. Naturally, he spoke in an annoying whine.

This could've been serious. If we lost the ice cream, we had no way of making money. If we didn't make some money, Ursula would go out of business. If Ursula went out of business, she'd hold me responsible. And, frankly, having an ANGRY polar bear holding me responsible for the collapse of her business didn't sound like a whole lot of fun.

Thankfully, at that moment, Shark popped up. 'I can't find the cones . . .' she began; and then she looked down at the three black-clad would-be robbers, yelled, 'SEALS!' and jumped out of the van.

'AAARGH! SHARK!' shrieked the octopus, jumping out of the way just in time.

'OOOF!' choked the vacuum cleaner, catching a POUNCING shark right in the motor and coughing up a large number of grubby coins.

'RUN!' shouted the dog-sheep-whatever, and they ran.

'Yay!' cheered the kids, shovelling the coins up and sharing them out.

'OK, kids, line up!' I yelled. 'Who's first?'

While they were sorting themselves out, I GRABBED a box of cones and a scoop. 'Open up the freezer, Shark,' I said, as she hopped back into the van; and then I took a proper look at her. 'What's that brown stuff on your nose?'

'It's not ice cream,' Shark said quickly. 'Definitely not chocolate. Anyway, we've got customers!'

By the time we'd served them all, they were very

happy customers indeed; and we were very
happy ice-cream sellers. I reckoned we'd
probably made more money in one stop than
Ursula had made in the last week. In fact,
some of the kids had come back for seconds.

I was just getting ready to pack up when
I noticed the first little girl—the one whose
coin the vacuum cleaner had SNATCHED—was
hanging round looking unhappy.

'You can't have eaten that already!' I said.

I'd just sold her an **extra-large** cone piled high with scoops of chocolate, banana, and peanut-butter flavours, but now her hands were empty.

She shook her head gloomily. 'Somebody stole it,' she said.

'Oh no!' I said. 'Who was it?'

The little girl shrugged. 'Don't know,' she said. 'Didn't see them. I just looked away for a moment, and someone SNATCHED the ice cream out of my hand and ran away. Really fast. By the time I turned round, they were gone.'

'Hmmm,' I said. 'Probably another kid. Doesn't sound like the three who tried to rob us, anyway. Can't imagine any of them going at that speed.'

'Nope,' she agreed, and then a worried look came into her big brown eyes, and she stood on tiptoes and whispered, 'You should probably go before they come back.'

'Who?' I asked. 'Those three goons? I don't think we'll be seeing them again. Shark chased them off good and proper.'

'That's true,' she agreed. 'But their boss isn't going to take that lying down.'

'Who?' I said.

'Their boss,' she repeated. 'Jimmy the Fridge.'

Oh. This was slightly more serious.

I'd heard of Jimmy the Fridge—a small-scale criminal gang-boss with a reputation for holding a grudge. Unless I wanted to feel that tentacle round my throat again, we needed to move quickly.

'OK, Shark . . .' I began, turning to her, and then stopped. 'What's that green stuff on your nose?'

'It's not ice cream,' Shark said quickly. 'Definitely not mint.'

I sighed. 'Come on,' I said. 'We've got to get out of here. Let's get Clive into gear and get going.'

'OK,' she said, and hopped out of the van. Then she hopped back in again. 'Who's Clive?'

'The horsey,' I reminded her.

'Oh, yeah,' she said, and HOPPED back out again.

Then she HOPPED back in again. 'Erm . . . where is the horsey?' she asked.

I looked out through where, in a less rubbish van, the windscreen would have been. Sure enough, the space between the shafts was completely empty.

Clive had GONE.

CHAPTER SEVEN

Ursula wasn't happy when I called her and told her that her horse had apparently been kidnapped.

'Don't move,' she growled down the phone at me. 'I'll be there in half an hour.'

It felt like the longest half hour I'd ever spent. I couldn't shift the thought that Jimmy the Fridge's gang might be on their way back with reinforcements, and I couldn't keep from getting edgy. Just the wind, RUSTLING the litter on the ground, was enough to make me jump, and Shark's constant JIGGLING began to get on my nerves.

'Can't you keep still?' I grumbled.

'Nope,' she said cheerfully. 'I'm a shark.

I have to keep moving. SEAL!' she added, and LEAPT out through the hatch. 'OW!' she continued a moment later, rubbing her nose.

'That's not a seal, Shark,' I said wearily. 'It's a tow-truck.'

'OK,' said Shark, climbing back into the van.

The tow-truck RUMBLED to a halt, and Ursula clambered out. I had no idea where she'd borrowed it from, and, frankly, at that moment I didn't care. I just wanted to get out of there before Jimmy the Fridge's crew returned. Without saying a word, she HITCHED up her old broken-down ice-cream van; and then she turned and leaned threateningly towards me.

I suddenly remembered what she'd said about holding me responsible for anything that went wrong.

'So,' she growled. 'No horse.' She leaned closer, and this time I detected a touch of trout among the other fishy aromas on her breath. 'You know who's to blame for this, don't you.'

'Er...well...I suppose you're, um, going to say I am...' I began. 'But if I could just...'

'PILBEAM!'

she roared suddenly, bringing her enormous paws down on the roof of the van so heavily that it SHOOK, and a dent appeared in the ceiling

above my head. I was beginning to understand how it had got so battered. 'Pilbeam's to blame!'

'Yes, Pilbeam,' I agreed hurriedly. 'That's just what I was going to say. It's all Pilbeam's... um... why do you think it's Pilbeam's doing?'

I'm not sure if she even heard me. She dropped on to all fours and began to pace round the van, roaring FURIOUSLY to herself about Pilbeam, and how he was determined to drive her out of business, and what she was going to do to him when she caught up with him. Frankly, it seemed a little unfair—Pilbeam was an obvious suspect, but it certainly wasn't an open-and-shut case. It was just as likely that Jimmy the Fridge's thugs had stolen Clive—but a good detective never jumps to conclusions. You examine the evidence; you look for clues; you never blame someone just because you don't like them.

Ursula's feud with Pilbeam, however, wasn't

my problem.

My problem was what she said next.

'And you two! You're fired! Get out of my van!'

I weighed my next words carefully. On one hand, we'd lost her horse—but on the other hand, according to her, that was a penguin's fault, not ours.

'OK,' I said. 'I'll admit that the Stuff hasn't gone entirely smoothly. It's not clear exactly what's gone wrong, but what is clear is that, right now, you need some Detectiving . . .'

Ursula stared. Then she glared, her eyes narrow little dots of anger. 'Detectiving?' she GROWLED. 'From you two? You couldn't even detective a whole horse being stolen from under your noses!'

I had to admit, she had a point. Then again, we had sold an awful lot of ice cream for her. So it seemed reasonable to show her our takings and say,

'Fair enough. We'll just take our fee and . . .'

She SPRANG up, front paws on the ledge of the serving hatch. If she'd leaned in any further I think my head would have disappeared inside her mouth.

'I'm not paying you a penny!' she growled, filling my nostrils with the exquisite scent of dead herring. 'And you can walk home! You!' she added, glaring at Shark.

'What's that pink stuff on your nose?'

'It's not ice cream,' Shark said quickly. 'Definitely not raspberry.'

Ursula roared and flung herself at Shark. Thankfully, the hatch was in the way, and while she was vainly struggling to squeeze her ample rear through, Shark and I ducked her thrashing claws, LEAPT out of the van, and scarpered as quickly as we could.

CHAPTER EIGHT

It was a long walk back to the office. I kept a sharp eye out for Jimmy the Fridge's gang until we were well out of the Inner West Side, but we had no further trouble; the most exciting thing to happen was Shark mistaking a litter bin for a seal. And that really wasn't very exciting, even the first time it happened. By the twenty-seventh, it had just got boring. At last, we found ourselves back outside the building.

'What's that noise?' Shark asked, as I pushed open the outer door.

'Well, about time!' I said looking inside. 'I've been telling the landlord for months that the hallway needs a spring clean.'

The noise was coming from a vacuum cleaner who was HAPPILY hoovering the floor just outside our office door, humming to himself as he did so.

'SEAL!' Shark yelped happily, throwing herself forward.

'No, Shark!' I said impatiently; and then three things happened at once.

The vacuum cleaner WHIRLED and SCOOTED backwards in a way that seemed oddly familiar.

A pygmy hippopotamus—about the size of a fat dog, or a particularly fluffy sheep—LEAPT out from behind us and shouted,

'Now!'

And an octopus holding a **very large** net dropped from the ceiling. Suddenly, we were **caught.**

'Hey!' Shark yelled. 'What do you think I am, a tuna?'

'Ha!' whined the vacuum cleaner. 'Not so smart now, are you?'

'Not you three again,' I said, more bravely than I felt. 'We've got no money, thanks to you, and no ice cream either, so you might as well let us out of this. I can't see what else you want.'

'Oh, can't you?' said the pygmy hippo, WADDLING smugly towards us, and leaning forwards so that his wide, flat nose almost touched mine. 'Where is it?'

For a moment I didn't know what to say. 'Where's what?' I managed eventually, feeling somewhat lost for words.

The hippo narrowed his eyes, which were frankly quite narrow enough to begin with. 'Don't play games with me, kid. You know what we're looking for.'

'I really don't have a clue,' I told him.

He narrowed his eyes some more, in a way that was probably meant to be menacing but actually just looked a bit stupid. 'I said, don't play games!'

'Awww,' said Shark. 'I like playing games. We could have a nice game of Find the Seal? What happens is, you hide a seal, and then . . .'

'Shut it!' roared the hippo, squinting at her.

'OK,' said Shark.

'Now,' said the hippo, 'we can do this the easy way, or the hard way. Ain't that right, Sucker?'

I bristled. Being TANGLED up in a net and threatened was bad enough; I wasn't going to let him get away with insulting me as well. 'Who are you calling "sucker"?'

The pygmy hippo un-narrowed its eyes for a moment and frowned at me in puzzlement.

'Him, of course,' he said.

'Yeah, me,' agreed the vacuum cleaner. ''Cos that's my name, see?' It lifted its nozzle threateningly, and pointed it at my face. 'Now,' he went on, 'are you going to tell us what you know, or do I have to suck it out of you?' His motor roared; I felt my hair RUSTLE as the nozzle moved closer.

'I keep telling you, I don't know anything!' I said desperately.

'I do!' said Shark cheerfully.

The pygmy hippo grinned. 'That's more like it. Tell me everything you know, fishbrain, or Sucker here gets to work on your friend's face.'

'OK,' said Shark. 'Um . . . you can't fit a bus inside a sleeping bag. There's no point in buying socks if you're a seahorse. Knees look funny. Crocodiles are not the same as potatoes. Bees . . .'

'What are you talking about?' the hippo snapped.

'You said to tell you everything I know,' said Shark. 'Bees can't water-ski. Toasters are more dangerous than sharks. If you fill an ambulance with jelly and then . . . OW!' she added, as the hippo **biffed** her on the nose. 'What did you do that for?'

'To shut you up,' the hippo GROWLED, and turned back to me. 'Last chance, kid. Tell me where it is.'

The nozzle drew closer, the whine grew louder, and I tried to make sense of what was happening. 'I have no idea what you're looking for!' I yelled in frustration.

As if in answer, a THUMP came from the other side of the office door.

The hippo froze. 'What was that? Hey, Sucker, shut up a minute, will you? Tracy, did you hear that?'

The octopus was already pressed against the door. 'I can hear something moving,' she said; and then jumped back as the THUMPING came again, louder.

'It's in there!' the hippo hissed excitedly. 'We've found it! Oh, boy, is the boss gonna be pleased with us!' He moved away from us, towards the door; Sucker did the same. 'Tracy!

Get the other net ready!'

I still had no idea what they were after, or why they thought it had anything to do with us, but I saw our chance to escape. Our captors' eyes were fixed on the door; for the moment, we were forgotten. As Tracy SHIMMIED up the wall, and Sucker and the hippo edged away from us, I raised my finger to my lips and then fed a section of the net into Shark's mouth, keeping it as taut as I could. She closed her teeth around it and the strands silently parted; I fed in another, and another, and the hole in the net grew bigger.

By this time, Tracy was poised above the door, another net STRETCHED wide and waiting, and Sucker was standing well clear of the doorway. From inside the office, the CLATTERING and THUMPING grew louder.

'Ready?' the pygmy hippo asked, one foot

on the door handle.

The octopus did what would have been a thumbs up, if she'd had any thumbs. 'Ready, Nigel!'

'And . . . now!' said Nigel the pygmy hippo, PUSHING the door open in a single movement.

Instantly, there was PANDEMONIUM as the desks BOUNDED out of the office, yipping and yelping. Unsure whether these newcomers were friends to play with or intruders to scare off, they settled for trying to do both at once.

Within moments, Knots and Hardwood were SQUEEZING Sucker between them in an enormous crushing hug, and Chip and Cedar, in full cry, were chasing Nigel up the stairs.

Meanwhile, Tracy had dropped from the ceiling, net OUTSTRETCHED. Whatever she'd thought she was going to catch, she'd clearly only been expecting one of them; unfortunately for her, she'd managed to get both Chunky and Trundle at once. With a yelp of alarm, they LEAPT in opposite directions, pulling the net tight and CATAPULTING her upwards. She hit the ceiling with a hard THUD, bounced off, and landed back on the net. Startled, the two desks LEAPT apart once more, turning the net into a trampoline again and throwing her straight up again. This time, she stuck for a moment, before peeling off and dropping back down, frightening the two desks, who LEAPT apart...

You get the picture. She was starting to turn orange, which I guessed was octopus for 'Please stop slapping me against the ceiling.'

Taking our chance, Shark and I SQUEEZED through the hole we'd made in our own net, and ran—or, at least, I ran. Shark hopped. Behind us, I could hear Sucker and Nigel bellowing FURIOUSLY after us as they tried to escape from the desks.

Out in the street, the low late-afternoon sun was DAZZLING. I turned away from it and we raced up the street, our shadows s t r e t c h i n g out ahead of us.

'Where are we going?' Shark wanted to know.

'Not sure,' I puffed. 'But wherever it is, we're going there quickly. Those desks won't hold them for long . . .'

Sure enough, moments later Sucker HURTLED out of the office building behind us.

'Stop!' he yelled.

'OK,' said Shark, and stopped.

'What are you doing?' I panted.

'I'm stopping,' she said.

'Well, don't!' I said. 'Keep going!'

'OK,' she said, and kept going.

I glanced over my shoulder. Through the sun's glare I could just make out Sucker, tearing up the street after us. Behind him, Nigel—with a DIZZY and BATTERED Tracy clinging to his back—galloped out of the building, gaining rapidly on Sucker and definitely going faster than Shark and me. I put on a BURST of speed, but squinting over my shoulder into the bright sunlight behind us, I could see it was hopeless; they were going to catch us.

That was when, behind them, the unicorn appeared.

CHAPTER NINE

Against my better judgement, I found myself stopping and staring. I couldn't see it clearly—it was just a black silhouette with the sun's bright halo shining around it like a golden crown, and the bright sunlight was making spots DANCE in front of my eyes—but there was nothing else it could have been. It was shaped like a magnificent horse, its head held high and proud, a single horn jutting out from its noble forehead. It was definitely a unicorn.

The thing is—unicorns don't exist.

Yes, I know all kinds of weird things happen in this crazy city, but one thing I'm sure of:

Unicorns.

Do.

Not.

Exist.

Yet here one was, large as life and—even in silhouette and through the dazzle-spots— twice as beautiful. It reared, and time seemed to freeze, as if the air itself had turned into pure enchantment. For just a moment, I forgot about everything else.

'Shark,' I whispered, 'do you see what that is?'

'Yep,' said Shark happily. 'It's a big goat.'

'It is not a goat!' I hissed, still trying not to break the wonder of the moment. 'It's a . . .'

And then two things happened, almost at once.

The first was that Jimmy the Fridge's thugs caught up with us. Since the unicorn was behind them, they hadn't been distracted by its startling magnificence, and frankly I'd been *so* distracted I'd forgotten all about them for just a second—no time at all, really, yet time enough for them to catch us.

I shook myself out of my trance, blinking away the spots, but already Tracy was reaching out for me, her body turning a triumphant shade of turquoise.

That was when the second thing happened: the unicorn LEAPT. Reaching us in a single bound, it picked Tracy up between its teeth and HURLED her onto the awning of a shop; kicked Nigel into Sucker so hard they ROLLED into the gutter; and in a rich, deep, commanding voice, said:

'Run!'

I ran.

Beside me, Shark hopped. Behind us, I could hear shouts of anger, and the sound of strong, steady hoofbeats fading in the opposite direction. I shot another glance over my shoulder. Nigel, still shouting, was struggling free from Sucker's hosepipe, while Tracy, orange once more, was CLAMBERING down from the awning. The unicorn was nowhere to be seen.

But the chase wasn't over yet. From far down the street, an engine coughed into life, and the biggest fork-lift truck I'd ever seen roared round the corner. It lowered its fork; Nigel, Tracy, and Sucker hopped on. It lifted them high; they scrambled into its cab as it turned towards us. There was no way we could outrun it.

Then I heard music. Heavenly, TINKLING, joyous music, as if my life had suddenly turned into a movie and some idiot had added the wrong soundtrack. Next second, a GLORIOUS sight: a gleaming blur of red and cream shot past the fork-lift and hurtled towards us. Pilbeam's van SCREECHED to a halt, and Darcy FLUNG the passenger door open.

'Oooh, goody!' said Shark. 'Could I have a 99, please?'

'Get in!' Darcy and I yelled simultaneously.

'OK!' Shark said cheerily, and got in.

I scrambled in behind her. The fork-lift was almost upon us, its fork-tips reaching low to slide under the van. I SLAMMED the door. The van JOLTED as the fork beneath us clanged against its underside.

'Go!' I shouted. Darcy stamped on the accelerator; the van's electric motor whined. My heart lurched as the back of the van began to lift. 'Faster!' I bellowed.

'Go, you stupid thing! Go!'

Darcy yelled,

pressing on the pedal with all her might.

With a jerk, and a loud, nasty, tearing, scraping sound, we LEAPT forward. There was a sudden stench of burning rubber as Darcy fought for control and we SCREECHED round the corner and away.

I gave Shark a hand with her seatbelt, and fastened my own. Then I leaned back in the seat and breathed out, a long, slow sigh of relief. 'That was too close,' I said. 'Thanks, Darcy.'

'Yeah, thanks,' agreed Shark. 'Can I have my 99 now?'

'No!' Darcy said sharply.

Questions began to flood into my head. 'How did you know to come and rescue us?'

Darcy looked straight ahead, eyes on the road. 'I didn't,' she said after a moment. 'I just happened to be passing. I've almost sold out of ice cream, and I'm heading back to Pilbeam's warehouse for some more. Lucky for you this road's on the way.'

I nodded. 'But then . . . how did you know to stop for us just now? I mean—you can't have even seen us till you overtook the fork-lift.'

She glanced over at me. 'You don't grow up

on the Inner West Side
without learning to recognize
Jimmy the Fridge's gang. If they're
chasing someone, that someone probably
needs help.'

I nodded again. 'Well, thanks again,'
I said. 'Don't suppose you know what they
want with us?'

She shook her head, eyes fixed on the road.
'Did they say anything?'

'Well, yeah,' I said. 'They were looking
for something—didn't tell us what, but kept
asking us where it was, as if they expected us
to know.'

'And then a big goat helped us get away,'
Shark said happily.

'A big goat?' Darcy asked.

'Yep,' Shark answered. 'A big goat with one
pointy horn.'

Darcy glanced at me, her expression

unreadable. 'Does she mean . . . a unicorn? Did you see it?'

I screwed up my eyes and peered at her. 'Unicorns don't exist. You know that, right?'

'Oh, yeah,' she said. 'Definitely. It's just . . . well, I like to think that maybe they do…'

Her voice tailed off, and the rest of the journey passed in silence.

CHAPTER TEN

Pilbeam's warehouse was a big red-brick building in a car park at the docks, with a sign above the door showing a big picture of a smiling Pilbeam under the words 'Pilbeam's Ice Creams'. The car park was surrounded by high walls on three sides, and the sea on the fourth.

'Where *is* Pilbeam?' I asked, as we pulled up in front of the huge double doors. 'I thought he was doing the ice-cream round with you?'

'He was just making sure I could drive the van without crashing it,' Darcy told me. 'You know, since it's my first day. Right now he'll be in his office next door, putting his flippers up while I do all the work.' She pressed a button on the dashboard, and the warehouse doors began to SLIDE open. 'And to be honest, I think he wanted to make Ursula feel bad. He made me drive round and round until we saw her tatty old van, and then he made me park near it and wait. He's not a very nice penguin.'

'Then why do you work for him?' Shark asked, as the doors finished SLIDING and the van glided through them.

Darcy shrugged. 'I need the money.' She hopped out of the van. 'Now: how about giving me a hand, since I saved your necks . . . ?'

'I don't have a neck,' Shark pointed out. 'I'm a shark.'

In spite of herself, Darcy smiled—just for a moment, but I definitely saw it. 'OK: I saved his neck, and your tail. So help me load up with flavours. Two tubs of vanilla; two of chocolate; and one of every other flavour till we run out of space in the van. Go!'

I got out of the van, Shark following behind me, and took a look round. A number of huge freezers stood around the warehouse, arranged in a fat crescent, leaving a wide circular space easily big enough for the van to turn in. Darcy was already opening freezers, lifting out tubs of ice cream, and carrying them to the van. I joined in, as did Shark, balancing the tubs on her nose, and in no time the van was loaded up and ready to go.

'Thanks, you guys,' said Darcy. 'I'll be back

in a few hours. You should be safe here for now, and when I've finished work we'll figure out what to do next.' She squinted at Shark. 'What's that orange stuff on your nose?'

'It's not ice cream,' Shark said quickly. 'Definitely not mango. Anyway, shouldn't you be going?'

Darcy sighed and shook her head. 'Don't let her eat all the ice cream, will you?' she said to me. Then she climbed into the van, and was gone.

I turned to Shark. 'Well, hopefully we should be safe here for a bit. There's not much to do in here, though.'

'We could look in the freezers,' Shark said hopefully. 'You know—for, um, clues. And exciting new flavours. But mostly for clues,' she added hurriedly, as I gave her a stern look.

The next few hours were boring. Really, really boring. We played I Spy for a bit, but that wasn't much fun because Shark's not terribly good at spelling. Then we played Ice Spy, which involved Shark sticking her nose into a freezer and me having to guess what flavour she definitely didn't have on her nose. Then Shark suggested a number of other games including Ice Pie, My Spy, and Mice Pie, all of which sounded interesting but turned out not to have proper rules and were, in fact, just excuses for Shark to help herself to more of Pilbeam's ice cream. And then . . .

'What's that noise?' said Shark.

'What noise?' I asked; and then I heard it, too. A sort of frantic SLAPPING sound, getting closer and closer. 'It's coming from outside,' I said, turning towards the door.

A moment later, with a cry of,

'HEEEELLLLLLLLP!'

Pilbeam dashed in,
SLIPPED, SKIDDED, SLAMMED
straight into my ankles,
and took my legs
out from under me.

'Wooooah!!' I yelled, toppling on top
of him just as a fully-grown polar bear sprang

through the doorway with a snarl. 'Ooof!' I
added, as she landed.

'SEAL!' yelped Shark, leaping forward
joyfully and biting Ursula on the bottom.

'ARRRRRRGGGGGGH!'
roared Ursula, kicking blindly out.
'OW!' yelped Shark, as the kick caught her
on the nose.

'Get off!' Pilbeam and I yelled together.

It went on like this for at least a minute before I managed to SQUEEZE myself, aching and bruised, out from under Ursula, dragging Pilbeam with me. I wasn't trying to rescue him; his beak had just got caught in my belt.

'What the heck is going on?' I demanded.

'She tried to kill me!' Pilbeam squawked, hiding behind my legs. 'She came to my office and ATTACKED me!'

'I never attacked you!' Ursula bellowed. 'I just got angry and yelled a bit, that's all! You've ruined me! You sell on my patch, you steal Darcy away from me, you kidnap my horse . . .'

'I didn't touch your scruffy old horse!' Pilbeam screeched. 'And it's not my fault if you can't hang on to your staff!'

'Hey! Hey!' I said, holding one hand out towards Ursula and using the other to pry Pilbeam off my trouser leg. 'Can we just calm it down a bit?'

'OK,' said Shark.

'I meant them, not you,' I told her.

'OK,' said Shark again. 'Does that mean I can be uncalm?'

'No!' I said. 'Let's all be calm. And quiet. Please?'

'Wait a minute!' Pilbeam squawked. 'What are you two doing in here, anyway? This is private property! You're trespassing!'

'We're hiding,' I said. 'Which is why it would be lovely if you could just be a bit quieter.'

'Hiding?' grunted Ursula. 'Who from?'

'Us!' said a cold voice.

I whirled. There, blocking the doorway, stood Nigel the pygmy hippopotamus, Tracy the octopus, and Sucker the vacuum cleaner. Behind them loomed the huge fork-lift truck who had chased us earlier; lifted high on its fork, it held a sinister figure.

Pilbeam emitted a frightened little squeak. 'That ... that's Jimmy the Fridge!'

CHAPTER ELEVEN

Jimmy the Fridge wasn't quite what I'd been expecting. For one thing, he wasn't a fridge.

He was a washing machine.

'It's a nickname,' he explained. 'Because I'm so cool.'

I said nothing and looked away. Maybe I should've been scared, but honestly, by this point I was just angry.

'**I said,**' he repeated more loudly, 'it's because I'm so cool.' When none of us said anything, he added. 'It's a joke. Y'know? Fridges keep things cool. But "cool" also means, like, really good. So it's funny.'

'It's about as funny as being kidnapped,' I told him.

He squinted menacingly at me, and made

a RATTLING noise with his soap drawer. 'Nobody's been kidnapped here,' he growled.

'I'd find that easier to believe,' I said, 'if any of us were free to move.'

Jimmy the Fridge glanced around at the four of us. Ursula was pinned against a freezer by the fork-lift truck who, it appeared, answered to the name of Prongs. I was being firmly held by Tracy the octopus, who'd wrapped one muscular tentacle round each of my limbs, with a fifth draped loosely round my throat and face. I could feel the suckers clinging lightly to my cheeks; it wasn't a pleasant sensation. Pilbeam, his beak taped up to stop him squawking, had been stuffed into a small wastepaper basket in the corner.

As for Shark, she was suspended by the tail from the ceiling. To make matters worse— or better, depending on your point of view—

Jimmy the Fridge's thugs hadn't been able to find a rope, so they'd used a bungee, which meant that Shark was bouncing up and down like a fish-flavoured yoyo. It kind of looked like fun, actually, and Shark was enjoying every second—except for the seconds when her head SMACKED against the tarmac.

So to get the full flavour of the following conversation, you really ought to imagine a large polar bear GROWLING angrily, a frustrated penguin making an 'Mmmmm! Mmmm! Mmmmm!' noise, and a shark going,

'Wheeeeeee—ow!—Wheeeeeee—ow!—Wheeeeeee—ow!' in the background.

'Anyway,' I said, 'what's a small-time criminal like Jimmy the Fridge doing, getting mixed up in the ice-cream trade?'

Jimmy glared FURIOUSLY at me, and his dial clicked up a notch from 'cool wash'. 'I ain't no small-time criminal,' he spat. 'Not any more. Sure, I wasn't always so law-abiding—I got my start laundering dirty money.' He leaned in, and again his soap drawer rattled. 'That's funny, see? 'Cos I'm a washing machine.'

He paused, waiting for a laugh. I didn't oblige, and after a moment, he continued. 'Anyway, I aim to be an honest businessman. And thanks to you, I ain't going to need to be involved in any, let's say, irregular activities any more.'

I frowned at him. 'Thanks to us . . . ? Oh, I get it. This has all been about forcing Ursula out of the ice-cream business so you can take over her territory!' Hearing this, Ursula ROARED more loudly and THRASHED her claws vainly at Prongs; I raised my voice over the noise. 'First you sent your goons to rob the ice-cream van; then you stole our horse. Now you're going to take over her patch and make a fortune selling your own ice cream. How'm I doing so far?'

Jimmy the Fridge chuckled. 'You're doing terribly, kid. Absolutely terribly. I got no interest at all in selling ice cream. No, I'm after something that's gonna make my fortune, and you guys are gonna help me get it.'

'Sorry—what?' I said. 'Firstly, I've got no idea what you're talking about, and secondly, you're not exactly putting me in a helpful frame of mind. I mean, aside from the fact that you've tied me up with an octopus and you're bouncing my best friend's head off the ground, you haven't even said "please".'

He chuckled again. 'I ain't asking; I'm telling.' There was a SCRAPING sound as he shuffled forwards and leaned towards me. 'You're gonna help me find the unicorn.'

'There's no such thing as unicorns,' I said.

Jimmy the Fridge's door slammed FURIOUSLY shut, and his dial clicked to 'spin'.

'Don't get smart with me, kid!' he bellowed.

'I know there's a unicorn; you know there's a unicorn. It's saved you twice now, so don't pretend otherwise!'

I shrugged. 'Yeah, OK ... Wait a minute. Twice?'

He RATTLED his soap drawer again, like someone clicking his teeth. 'Yeah, twice. An hour or so back, outside your office. And this morning, when my, ehm, friends here were coming back to have another go at, um, inspecting your ice-cream van.'

'Yeah,' chipped in Tracy from behind me, tickling my ear unpleasantly. 'We was just coming back to teach you a lesson, when suddenly, there's this unicorn, admiring itself in a shop window!'

'That's right,' agreed Nigel. 'It looked kind of gloomy for a moment, but as it gazed at its reflection, it seemed to fill with—'

'MAGIC!' Sucker chipped in.

'I was gonna say confidence,' Nigel said. 'But, yeah. It was kind of like magic. It stood up tall, and threw its head back, and neighed in this deep, majestic voice.'

'Then it saw us,' Tracy added. 'It neighed again, and said, "You're not going to try robbing that ice-cream van again, are you?" And when I said, "yeah, what are you going to do about it," it kicked me so hard I got knotted round a lamppost!'

'None of us really wanted to tangle with it after that,' whined Sucker. 'So we went and told the boss.'

'And of course,' said Jimmy the Fridge, 'that was when I had my brainwave. A real 1200 rpm genius idea. As far as we know, that unicorn is the only one in the world. So just imagine what people would pay to SEE it! To STROKE it! To RIDE on it! Why, once I've caught that unicorn, I'm gonna be the richest washing machine in the world!'

'Good for you,' I said. 'But what's that got to do with us?'

Again, he RATTLED his soap drawer. 'You're gonna tell us where to find it,' he said.

I shrugged. 'Sorry, Jimmy. I don't know anything about the unicorn. I didn't even know it existed ninety minutes ago, and to be honest, I'm still not a hundred per cent convinced it does. I can't help you.'

He chuckled, and one by one his gang joined in. It wasn't a pleasant sound.

'I think you can,' he said. 'See, that unicorn is looking out for you. It can't be a coincidence it's got you out of a jam twice. And here you are, in danger. I reckon it's gonna come and help you.'

I didn't like the sound of that. 'In danger? Are you threatening us?'

Jimmy the Fridge chuckled again. 'Oh,

you're not in danger from me, kid. I'm a respectable businessman. But it's getting dark.' He lowered his voice. 'And bad things happen at night.'

'Look,' I said desperately, 'I don't know anything about this unicorn. Maybe it did rescue us twice, but that's got to be just a coincidence . . .'

'I don't believe in coincidences, kid,' he said, backing away. 'Come on, Prongs.'

As Prongs moved suddenly backwards, Ursula roared her **loudest roar** and THREW herself at Jimmy the Fridge. But before she reached him, the vacuum cleaner stretched out his hose and I realized there was something attached to the end.

'Ursula, look out!' I yelled, but too late. The vacuum cleaner's motor whined, kicking from 'suck' to 'blow'. There was a noise, somewhere between 'POP' and 'PFFFFFFT', only just audible over the ROARING of both vacuum motor and polar bear. Ursula paused in mid-leap; staggered; fell.

'Ursula!'

I yelled again,

and rounded on Jimmy the Fridge. 'What've you done to her?'

If washing machines could smile, Jimmy would've done. As it was, he just made a gentle rinsing sound. 'Tranquilliser dart, kid. Enough sedative in it to knock out ... well, a polar bear, as it happens. She'll wake up in about ten minutes.' His voice dropped to a threatening undertone. 'Assuming nothing gets to her sooner, and stops her ever waking up again.'

'What do you mean?' I demanded, but already Prongs was scooping up Jimmy the Fridge. Tracy FLUNG me roughly across the warehouse and scrambled aboard, closely followed by Sucker and Nigel. As I picked myself up they cut Shark down; she fell with a 'Wheeeeeee—OW!!!!!' and remained for a moment standing on her head before slowly toppling over sideways.

'I don't know how that unicorn knows when you're in trouble,' Jimmy the Fridge went on, as Prongs reversed towards the doorway. 'But you better hope it don't let you down this time. We'll be waiting outside to grab it, see, when it comes to save you. Once we've got it all safe in a cage, we'll come back and save you ourselves.'

'You're making a mistake,' I said desperately. 'We honestly don't know anything about the unicorn. There's no way he's going to even know we're in danger, let alone come and save us.'

Jimmy the Fridge cackled unpleasantly, as he and his gang slowly backed out through the door. 'Is that so? Well, better hope you're wrong, kid. Otherwise—we'll be back in half an hour to pick up the pieces.'

CHAPTER TWELVE

Shark sat up, and slowly got to her tail. 'That was fun!' she said.

'No, Shark, it wasn't,' I told her. 'They captured us, and threatened us, and now they've left us alone with an unconscious polar bear and a penguin in a bin, to face some kind of unknown danger.'

'Oh,' said Shark. She scratched her head with one fin. 'But I got to go "wheeeeee!" on a BOINGY thing. That was fun.'

I sighed. 'If Jimmy the Fridge was telling the truth, it's not safe to stay here. So we need to get away; but we don't have a car, and I can't possibly carry Ursula—she's too heavy for me.'

'I could carry her,' Shark volunteered cheerfully.

'Shark,' I reminded her, 'you don't have any arms.'

'Oh, yeah,' Shark said. 'I forgot.'

'Mmmm!' said Pilbeam. 'Mmmmm!!!'

'I was getting to you,' I told him, pulling him out of the wastepaper basket and starting to untape his beak.

mmmm!

'This is all your fault!' he squawked, before I'd even finished getting the tape off. 'You and that bear! I'll sue! I'll have you arrested! I'll mmmmm! Mmmmmm! Mmmmmmmm!!!' he continued, as I taped his beak back up again.

'Sorry, Pilbeam,' I told him, 'but I need to focus.'

I leaned over Ursula. She was breathing deeply, and snoring gently. I reckoned we'd be very, very lucky indeed if she was awake in ten minutes. But then, if we were lucky, we wouldn't be in this mess in the first place.

'Maybe we could . . .' I began. I didn't really know what I was going to say; I was just hoping that by the time I reached the end of the sentence I'd have figured it out. But as it happened, I never reached the end of the sentence, because just then I heard a noise.

It was an oddly familiar noise: a sort of SNAP, but with a hint of SPROINGGG.

'What was that?' I asked.

'Mmm!' said Pilbeam, tugging at the tape with his flippers.

Shark listened, all the senses of a mighty hunter of the sea on full alert. She scanned the warehouse; sniffed the air; listened again. Then she turned to me.

'Dunno,' she said with a shrug. 'Shall we play a game while we're waiting for Ursula to wake up?'

The noise came again. It was strangely mechanical, like something being opened or shut with a strong spring. I knew the sound, I was sure of it. I'd heard it often, but here, it was out of place; wrong. Threatening.

It came a third time, and this time it was louder. Closer. Another sound came in answer, and another. Whatever it was, there was more than one of them. The sounds grew, in volume and in number.

Whatever they were, they were getting nearer and **nearer** to the huge double doors of the warehouse.

'Try and wake Ursula,' I said. 'I'll see if there's another way out.'

'OK,' said Shark, and she leaned over the slumbering bear and yelled,

'WAKEY WAKEY!'

Next to her, Pilbeam began to peck at Ursula, JABBING her gently with his beak. I wasn't sure if he was being helpful, or just doing something he'd always wanted to do but had never dared while the bear was awake.

Ursula didn't stir.

I scanned the warehouse. Above a row of freezers on one side hung a large window; through it the sunset was casting pale golden beams into the room, turning the space where we stood into an island of soft light in the dim evening grey. There was no sign of another door, though. I moved through the first row of freezers, into the blackness behind them, wondering if there might be a way out at the back—and stopped, rooted to the spot, as something moved. Something big, far back, in the darkness, hidden behind the next row, or the row after that.

I stepped back from the shadows. The sunset was still smearing bright streaks of orange and violet across the sky, but the light was fading fast. A sharp sea breeze was blowing through the doorway. I told myself that was what was giving me goose pimples;

but the truth was, I didn't like this situation. I didn't like it at all.

'There's something in here with us,' I said. 'Back there, behind the freezers. Something big, and alive.'

'Mmmm!' said Pilbeam.

'OK,' said Shark. 'What do we do?'

'I think we should get out of here,' I said.

At the entrance to the warehouse, something moved. Something small. No— not something; some things. Lots of things, SHUFFLING towards us in the falling night, blocking our exit. I moved closer to Shark, Pilbeam, and the still-unconscious Ursula.

The things—whatever they were—spread out as they entered, keeping a cautious distance like hyenas preparing to circle their prey. I caught sight of a glow, like two stripes burning orange in the gloom.

Then came that sound,
that
SNAP with a
hint of
SPROINGGG,
and the glow faded.

Suddenly, I knew what they were. Though I was right next to Shark, I took no comfort; for these were enemies much, much deadlier than any shark.

We were surrounded by TOASTERS.

CHAPTER THIRTEEN

Not all toasters are deadly, of course. Buy yourself a domesticated toaster and look after it properly, and it'll be your friend for life.

These toasters had not been looked after properly. Most of them had probably been abandoned years ago—dumped by the roadside when their owners replaced them with a newer model. Left to fend for themselves, they'd gone wild; formed a pack that preyed on anything they could find.

And now, they'd found us.

Or, rather, Jimmy the Fridge and his mob had found them and set them on us. SNAPPING, SNARLING, POPPING their bread racks, the savage little kitchen appliances circled us in the gloom, looking for weak spots. Sparks SPAT from their faulty heating elements, like tiny stars shooting across the night sky. Some of them had metal knives jammed into their slots; if any of them touched us, we were toast.

'What do we do?' Shark asked. It was the first time I'd ever heard her sound nervous.

'Jimmy the Fridge'll be back,' I said, sounding more confident than I felt. 'He's just trying to scare us into co-operating.'

'Are we scared enough to co-operate yet?' she asked.

'I think we probably are,' I admitted, and raised my voice. 'Mr the Fridge? You there?'

There was no answer but the rising wind, the crashing of the waves, and the snapping and CRACKLING of the faulty toasters as they circled us, drawing ever nearer. From outside came a distant click and a dim gleam, as the lights in the car park came on, giving me just enough light to see by as the daylight finally failed.

'Mmmmm!' said Pilbeam, nudging me with his beak. Without taking my eyes off the toasters, I ripped the tape off; however annoying he was, we were going to have to work together. 'Bear!' he hissed at once, jabbing at Ursula again. 'Wake up, you stupid bear! Wake up!'

Ursula stirred, groaning. 'Wha's happ'nin'?' she asked, in a bleary voice.

'Get up!' Pilbeam said.

'Don't make any sudden movements,' I warned her. 'We're being attacked by toasters.'

'Ooooh,' she said. 'I'll havva cr . . . cr . . . crrrrumpet, pleeez.'

'No,' I hissed. 'Wild toasters.'

She sat up, rubbing her eyes. 'Oh. Still

dark. Not brickfost . . . brockfist . . . urrr . . . breakfast, then?'

'Hopefully not,' I said. 'If it is, we're on the menu.'

She snorted, and staggered to her feet. 'Polabear'sh . . . norr on the menn-yoo . . . Ooof,' she added, falling over.

'Get up!' Pilbeam insisted, kicking her with one feeble flipper.

'Save your strength,' I told her. 'You're still groggy from the dart.'

'Don' play darts,' she muttered, rolling over. A couple of toasters, who'd got a little close for comfort, LEAPT back for fear of getting crushed.

'Should we **biff** them on the nose?' Shark asked me.

'I don't think they have noses,' I told her, crouching and feeling the warehouse floor for something—anything—I could use as a weapon. There was nothing. I drew as close to Shark as I could. 'I think this might be it, Shark,' I said. 'I can't see how we're going to get out of this one.'

The toasters were getting braver. Some of them began to make little half-dashes towards us. Any second now, they'd decide we were in no position to fight back, and then we'd be done for; as soon as one drew first blood, the whole pack would be upon us.

That was when I realized I could hear another noise, rising under the SNAPPING of the toasters: something hard striking the floor, getting faster and more rhythmic, like something picking up speed as it ran through the empty spaces between the freezers. Shark and I glanced at each other, hardly daring to hope; the toasters SNARLED and HOWLED uneasily. From the darkness at the back of the warehouse, something came galloping towards us. A pale shape bloomed from the shadows. Head held high, horn piercing the air, the unicorn rose magnificently over the freezers.

Pilbeam's beak fell open in astonishment.

'Yay!' said Shark. 'It's the big goat!'

Sparks flew from the majestic creature's hooves as they struck the concrete in front of us. The unicorn kicked backwards, SCATTERING the toasters behind him, and tossed his mane proudly.

'Quickly!' he boomed. 'Climb on my back!'

'OK!' mumbled Ursula, getting to her feet and collapsing onto her bottom again.

'You'll never carry us all!' I protested.

'Yeah,' agreed Shark. 'We're going to need a bigger goat.' She turned to me, concerned. 'I'm right, aren't I? We're going to need a bigger goat.'

'Just you and the penguin, child,' the unicorn said, his dimly-lit face almost shining in the gloom, and for a moment I felt a strange connection between us, as if we already knew one another. 'The bear is too heavy, and we will need to be swifter than I can run with a shark on my back. But fear not—help for your friends will come, and soon.'

The toasters JABBERED and CLATTERED wildly, sensing the imminent loss of their prey. One of the braver ones darted at me, sparks spitting from it, but the unicorn LASHED out with one hoof and sent it skittering across the warehouse floor and into the shadows. Enraged, several more HOWLED and EDGED closer, keeping just out of reach.

'Hurry up!' Pilbeam squawked, flapping FURIOUSLY, as if he'd forgotten he couldn't fly.

'On my back, child!' the unicorn repeated urgently. 'You and the penguin! They see you as the weakest; they'll try to separate you from us if you do not get out of reach!'

That made sense. Even a toaster was going to think twice about attacking Shark, until it was sure the others would back it up; and as for Ursula—who by now was sitting up again—she looked capable of disembowelling a small kitchen appliance in her sleep. The unicorn, meanwhile, could clearly take care of himself. The weak spots in our group were Pilbeam and me.

By the time I'd finished working all that out, I was sitting safely on the unicorn, out of reach of the toasters, Pilbeam tucked in front of me. Well—I say 'safely', but have you ever tried clutching a penguin and sitting bareback on a unicorn while it fights off a horde of vicious toasters? It's not easy holding on, let me tell you.

The toasters were ENRAGED now. All caution forgotten, they rushed us, their elements glowing, their springs SNAPPING and POPPING madly. Pilbeam shrieked in fright, trembling so hard I almost dropped him. 'Keep still, you idiot!' I yelled over the clattering of hooves, and the frantic, hungry baying of our attackers.

For a moment, I thought we'd had it. The unicorn, though, was undaunted; he kicked, stamped, trampled, lashed out as our enemies dashed and darted at us. With every kick another toaster left the ground to crash against the wall, smash into a freezer, or soar, sparking and sputtering, into a dark corner. He LEAPT and danced around them, keeping them away from Shark and Ursula, edging closer to the open door.

But a glance through the door—even from the back of a furiously-fighting unicorn—was enough to tell me there was no escape that way.

'They're waiting out there!' I shouted. 'Jimmy the Fridge and his gang!'

And that was when things got worse. Jimmy's gang were looking away from the door, clearly expecting the unicorn to come from the road outside—all except Nigel, whose little flappy ears had clearly caught the commotion, and whose bright little piggy eyes spotted us in the doorway. 'It's in the warehouse already!' he yelled.

'Prongs!' Jimmy the Fridge ordered. 'Get in there and scoop that unicorn up!'

'We've got to get out of here!' Pilbeam screeched.

'There isn't another way out!' I shouted.

'Fear not, child and penguin!' the unicorn boomed. He spun on his hooves and kicked out with both hind legs, hard and fast, again and again. Toasters flew through the air, snarling and jabbering angrily—though I'm almost sure I heard one shout, 'Wheeeeeee!' With a splintering crash, they smashed through the window, SHATTERING it into tiny fragments that rained outwards.

'Be of stout heart!' the unicorn went on, wheeling in a wide arc and pointing himself at the night outside. 'And hold on with all your might!'

Next thing, we were GALLOPING at full speed across the warehouse, with the remaining toasters in full cry after us. Behind us, Prongs burst through the doors, and wheeled round in pursuit.

'Wooooaaaaah!!!!' I yelled; and Pilbeam screamed as the unicorn LEAPT, his hooves striking the ground, the roof of a freezer, the window-ledge, propelling us onwards.

Then we were airborne.

CHAPTER FOURTEEN

Even as we landed outside in the darkness, there was chaos.

Already Prongs was reversing out of the warehouse, yelling, 'It got out! It got out!'

'Get after it, you nitwit!' Jimmy the Fridge hollered.

The unicorn didn't break stride, but ran for the gates to the car park. Prongs, headlights blazing, scooped up the rest of the gang and chased after us.

'What about Shark and Ursula?' I shouted. 'They're still in there with the rest of the toasters!'

'Fear not!' the unicorn boomed. 'Behold! Help is on its way!'

Sure enough, as we raced through the gates towards the road, I saw headlights sweeping towards us. I just had time to see Darcy's startled face through the windscreen before she was past us and heading for the double doors.

I glanced behind me; Prongs and the gang hadn't even slowed at the sight of Darcy. Clearly they were only interested in catching the unicorn.

The unicorn, for his part, clearly was not interested in being caught. Head forward, ears flat, he *RACED* away, with Pilbeam and me holding on for dear life. Through unfamiliar streets we ran, twisting and turning till I had no idea how far we'd travelled, all with Jimmy the Fridge's gang on our tail—never gaining on us, but never falling behind either.

We'd made so many U-turns I was feeling slightly DIZZY by the time we rounded a corner and entered a long, straight, tree-lined road, dimly lit by streetlights.

It took me a second to realize the road was a dead end. At the far end stood a high wall. Another glance behind me showed that Prongs and the others had reached the corner. We were trapped.

'There's no way out!' I shouted.

The unicorn ignored me. It galloped faster, ever faster. From behind me came the victorious shouts of our pursuers as they realized they had us.

The unicorn did not slow. And I realized that, though the wall was too high for him to leap, he was going to try. We weren't going to make it. I braced for impact. In front of me, Pilbeam SQUEAKED in terror.

In the darkness, I hadn't seen the gap in the wall: the opening to an alleyway, wide enough for us but too narrow for Prongs. The unicorn slipped through it and slowed to a canter as, behind us, the gang's shouts of TRIUMPH turned to yells of RAGE.

'Yes!' I cried, punching the air. 'That was amazing!'

'But where do we go now?' Pilbeam clucked anxiously. 'They'll be looking for us, won't they? We've got to get as far away as possible! There's a train leaving the city at midnight ...'

'Fie upon you, penguin!' boomed the unicorn. 'Flee, when we have friends still in need of help? Never!'

'He's right,' I said. 'We've got to get back to Shark and the others.'

Although the unicorn had carried us for what felt like miles, the twisting and turning of our route meant that we hadn't come far, as the crow flies. Soon we were trotting in through the gates to the warehouse car park, just as the ice-cream van drove out through the huge double doors. The unicorn TROTTED to meet it; I slipped off his back as we came to a halt. The gates swung silently shut behind us.

Pilbeam had been unusually silent for most of the ride, but seeing Ursula in his precious van brought him back to his normal overbearing self.

'Daisy!' he snapped, as I lifted him down.

'It's "Darcy", Mr Pilbeam,' Darcy reminded him wearily, getting out of the van.

'Whatever! The point is, what's that bear doing in my van?'

Darcy took a deep breath. 'I rescued her from a pack of ferocious toasters,

Mr Pilbeam,' she said.

'So?' said Pilbeam rudely. 'There aren't any toasters left now, are there?'

'No, Mr Pilbeam,' Darcy said. 'They ran off.'

'So get the bear out of my van!' Pilbeam said. 'Now, Dulcie!'

Darcy sighed, and turned to Ursula; but Ursula was already climbing out. She was clearly still a little woozy, but seemed almost recovered from the dart's effects.

'What happened?' she GROWLED.

'We got rescued,' I told her, with a sideways look at Darcy, 'but I'm not sure how. Maybe someone could explain a couple of things—like how you found us, and what a unicorn is doing actually existing?' I glanced at the proudly-standing unicorn, and back to Darcy—and then back at the unicorn again. The lights which lit the car park, although not terribly bright, were giving me my first clear look at his face, and there was something familiar about it. Very familiar.

I squinted at him, imagining the proud, noble stance slumping into a hunched and depressed posture; imagining the bright eyes dulled by despondency and the bright clean coat darkened by the grime of the city; imagining the horn gone from his forehead.

'Clive?' I asked hesitantly.

The unicorn looked down at me kindly. 'No longer, child. Once, yes, I was Clive the humble horse—lowly and despised. But since the miracle, I am transformed. Now I am a unicorn, and Clive is no name for a beast such as myself. Henceforth I shall be known as . . .'—He paused, and looked round dramatically, striking an impressive pose—'Dave!'

I looked at Darcy. She shrugged.

'Sorry,' I said. 'Just to get this straight—you think "Clive the unicorn" isn't a very good name, so you're calling yourself, "Dave the unicorn"? How is that any better?' As he opened his mouth to reply, I went on, 'Actually, never mind that now. What I really want to know is: what miracle? How did you turn into a unicorn?'

Clive—or Dave—held his head high, as if looking to the stars for answers. 'Why it happened, I know not,' he said. 'How it was that the universe chose me for this honour, may always remain a mystery. But what I can tell you is this: earlier today, when the van was ATTACKED, I was frightened. And though your companion fought them off, I feared that the ruffians would return. Then I thought to myself, "Every day I trudge the streets, pulling this heavy load, for but little reward. Should I also put myself in the path of danger for an employer who cares so little for me?"'

Ursula stared at him. 'Wait a minute!' she GROWLED. 'Are you telling me you're my horse, but now you're a unicorn?'

I shook my head disbelievingly. 'Didn't you just hear him say he was Clive?'

'Yeah, but I didn't know my horse was called Clive. I thought it was Colin, or Elizabeth, or something.'

Darcy shook her head. 'You and Pilbeam—

you're as bad as each other!'

'Anyway,' I said, 'Clive—sorry, Dave—you were saying?'

'It took me several minutes to loosen the harness which bound me,' the unicorn continued, 'but at last I was able to wriggle free. And then, head down, I ran, blindly and fearfully. Hardly, though, had I left the van behind me when I was sorely afflicted with a pain both sudden and intense, as if my very skull were SPLITTING. Thinking I had been attacked, I ran on, agonized and terrified—until suddenly, looking up for a moment, I caught sight of my reflection in a shop window, and I stopped in wonder at the change which had come upon me. No longer was I Clive the lowly carthorse. I had been transformed into the noble unicorn you see before you!'

'You know,' I whispered to Darcy, 'I'm sure he didn't use to talk like this.'

'He does go on a bit, doesn't he,' she agreed. 'But he means well.'

'And even as I wondered at my good fortune,' Clive continued, 'I beheld the same ruffians who had so frightened me. But I was no longer afraid, for if a horse can become a unicorn, surely he can do many mighty things! So I KICKED them until they ran away.'

There was a moment of silence once he'd finished.

'Well, I suppose that's the mystery solved,' I said.

'And I've got my horse back,' said Ursula.

'Oooh, is the horsey back?' said Shark, popping up from the serving hatch of the van. **'Hello, horsey!'**

'Hello, fishy,' said Clive.

Shark looked at him. 'You're not the horsey,' she said. 'You're the big goat.'

'The big goat is actually a unicorn, Shark,' I said. 'And the unicorn used to be the horsey.'

'Oh,' said Shark. 'OK.'

'And,' I added, 'what's that yellow stuff on your nose?'

'It's not ice cream,' Shark said quickly. 'Definitely not banana.'

Pilbeam squawked indignantly, and opened his beak to say something, but whatever it was remained unheard. Because just at that moment there came the sound of an engine. We were caught in the sudden glare of bright lights, and Jimmy the Fridge's voice rang out.

'I told you, kid! I told you the unicorn would come to rescue you. And I told you I'd get that unicorn. It's mine now, and there's nothing you can do about it!'

CHAPTER FIFTEEN

I walked up to the gate. 'These gates are pretty solid,' I said. 'You can't get in.'

Jimmy the Fridge SNIGGERED unpleasantly. 'And you can't get out. Ain't none of you getting out of here without handing that unicorn over.'

I looked behind me at the worried faces of Shark, Darcy, Ursula, and Clive, and at the car park surrounded by high walls which opened to the sea. That meant Shark and Pilbeam would have no problem escaping, and polar bears are pretty good swimmers too. There was no way, though, that they could carry a fully-grown unicorn—especially one who shouldn't get his horn wet. And that was without worrying about Darcy or me. I couldn't see any way out.

Or could I? I realized that I'd just thought something weird—as if the hidden part of my mind, the detectiving part, had figured something out and was trying to tell me. I thought hard; then it hit me.

Why did I think that Clive shouldn't get his horn wet?

I looked back at him again. He was still standing proudly, unafraid even though this gangster and his mob had come to capture him. But now, in the harsh glare of Prongs's headlights, I could see him much more clearly than before—properly clearly, for the first time—and I realized that something was bothering me. Something about his horn.

I stared at it; I'd seen something like it— something really like it—recently. What was it making me think of? Something that would be ruined if it got wet . . .

And then I got it, and it all made sense to me, and I knew how we were getting out of this.

'So tell me, Jimmy,' I said. 'How do you know that's actually a unicorn?'

'Easy,' he snorted. 'It's a horse with a horn growing out of its forehead.'

I nodded. 'Right,' I said. 'And, a unicorn's horn—how tough is it?'

'Oh, amazingly tough, I reckon,' Jimmy the Fridge said. 'There wouldn't be much that could damage a unicorn's horn.'

'No,' I agreed. 'So—just for instance—a shark couldn't BITE through it?'

'Nah,' he scoffed. 'No way.'

'OK,' I said. 'Let's put that to the test. Hey, Shark!' I called, turning. 'See if you can bite through Clive's horn!'

'OK,' said Shark; and before anyone could move she LEAPT and, with a soft squishy crunch, BIT the horn clean off Clive's forehead.

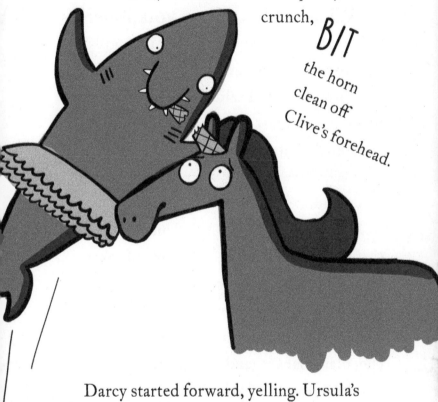

Darcy started forward, yelling. Ursula's mouth fell open. Jimmy the Fridge went into a furious spin cycle.

'Mmmm,' said Shark, liquid ice cream

dribbling from between her jaws.

'Chocolate, banana, and peanut-butter! Yum.'

'What the heck have you done?!'
Jimmy the Fridge shrieked. 'My unicorn!
You've ruined my unicorn!'

'Sorry, Jimmy,' I said. 'It's not a unicorn. It
never was. It's just a horse with an ice-cream
cone stuck to its forehead.'

'I am?' Clive said, his voice suddenly small
and afraid.

'I'm afraid so, Clive,' I told him. 'You said
that when you ran away, you weren't looking
where you were going, remember? And you
were running with your head down? Well, you
ran straight into a freshly-scooped ice cream—
chocolate, banana, and peanut-butter flavours.
The kid we sold it to thought someone had
stolen it, but I'm guessing you just collided
with it by accident. Ursula probably uses
real—and very sticky—peanut-butter, sticky

enough to stick the cone to your head.'

Ursula nodded dazedly.

'But, wait!' Clive said, suddenly hopeful again. 'That doesn't explain the blinding pain when the horn grew from within my head! I know I didn't imagine that!'

I shook my head reluctantly. 'No, you didn't imagine it; but it wasn't caused by a unicorn's horn bursting through your skull. It was BRAIN-FREEZE from having a cone full of cold ice cream RAMMED against your forehead. It could've happened to anyone.'

As if a genuine unicorn enchantment had fallen away from him, Clive slumped. His head drooped; his shoulders sank; and when he spoke again, it was no longer in the ringing tones of Dave the unicorn, but the mournful voice of Clive, the gloomy horse who had pulled Ursula's ice-cream van. 'So... I'm not a real unicorn?'

'GAAAARRGH!!!!'

roared Jimmy the Fridge.

'AAARGARRGRRRRAAAAAH!!!! YOU IDIOTS! YOU'VE WRECKED EVERYTHING!'

'Excuse me,' I said. 'I haven't wrecked anything. I've worked out what happened, that's all. It's what us detectives do.'

'I haven't wrecked anything either,' Shark put in. 'And I haven't worked out what happened. What happened?'

'What happened,' Jimmy growled, 'is that I nearly had a unicorn, and now you've turned it back into a useless horse! How am I going to get rich now?'

I shrugged. 'Not my problem. Maybe you could try getting a job?'

Jimmy the Fridge growled, and RATTLED his soap drawer FURIOUSLY. But then his dial flipped to 'Drain', and, with a funny GURGLING noise, he seemed to sag.

'OK, kid,' he growled. 'You win. This time. But I ain't gonna forget how you and that fish meddled in my business. You better watch out if you ever cross my path again. Let's go home, Prongs.'

Prongs backed away from the gate. His headlights swept the road as he turned, and then he ACCELERATED away, and Jimmy the Fridge's gang was gone.

I turned back to the assembled company with a satisfied smile. 'Well,' I said, 'we found the missing horse, and solved the mystery of the unicorn...'

'But what was it doing in my warehouse?' Pilbeam squawked, glaring at Clive, who shrank back nervously.

I glanced at Darcy. 'I think when Clive thought he'd been turned into a unicorn, and found himself being hunted by mobsters, he asked his only friend to hide him.'

Clive nodded gloomily. 'I knew Jimmy the Fridge was trying to catch me, so I thought I'd better hide. And Darcy's the cleverest person I know, so I thought she'd come up with a good hiding place for me.'

Darcy nodded. 'So I suggested the warehouse. But Clive thought Jimmy the Fridge might come after you, too. So we decided to come back here via your office, just in case.'

I smiled wryly. 'Lucky for us you did.'

She smiled back. 'Luck had nothing to do

with it, buster. Anyway, once you were out of danger, Clive ran ahead of us and hid in the warehouse ... but I guess Jimmy worked out I was helping Clive, and since I was driving Pilbeam's van, he must've figured paying Pilbeam a visit would be a good idea.'

Pilbeam almost EXPLODED. 'So, what you're telling me, Daphne—'

'My name's Darcy,' she reminded him quietly.

'I DON'T CARE! The point is, you hid a unicorn in my warehouse, even though dangerous gangsters were chasing it! And you helped a boy and a shark, even though the gangsters were chasing them too! I'm very disappointed in you, Dixie. We'll talk tomorrow. Now put that van back in the warehouse and go home!'

I could tell Darcy wanted to argue, but I could also tell she didn't want to get fired.

'Yes, Mr Pilbeam,' she said sadly. She climbed into the van, started it up, and drove it into the warehouse. The doors closed behind her.

'I think you're being a bit hard on her,' I said.

'Yeah,' said Shark. 'She's nice.'

'I don't care what you two think!' Pilbeam snapped. 'Get off my property! And you, bear! And that moth-eaten excuse for a horse!'

Ursula reared up. 'Why, you . . . !'

Pilbeam squeaked and ducked behind me, grabbing my legs.

'Hey!' I said. 'How can I get off your property when you're holding on to me?'

'KEEP THAT BEAR AWAY FROM ME!'
Pilbeam squawked.

'I OUGHT TO USE YOU AS A
BASKETBALL!'
Ursula roared.

'What's that noise?' asked Shark.

'That's Pilbeam and Ursula having an argument,' I told her, trying to pry Pilbeam free from my trouser leg.

'No,' Shark said. 'The banging noise.'

And then I heard it too. A THUMPING sound, and a muffled yelling. And ...

'What's that burning smell?' Shark asked.

I looked at the warehouse. A trail of smoke was coming from the broken window. The doors were closed. And under the sounds of a penguin and a bear YELLING at each other,

I could hear a voice. Darcy's voice,

'Mr Pilbeam!'
she was calling.

'I can't get the
door open!'

The warehouse was on fire. And Darcy was trapped inside.

CHAPTER SIXTEEN

'Shut up, you two!' I yelled, so loudly that Pilbeam and Ursula actually shut up. 'Look!'

'My warehouse!' Pilbeam squeaked, letting go of me and starting forward. 'My ice cream!'

'Never mind your warehouse!' I said urgently. 'Darcy's trapped in there!'

Pilbeam looked at me blankly. 'Who?'

Ursula ROARED, and I had to get in her way to stop her swiping at him. 'Darcy! The girl who drives your van!'

Pilbeam gasped. 'My van!'

'We've got to save her!' I said. 'Ursula! See if you can get the doors open!'

Ursula flung herself at the doors and heaved. 'No use,' she grunted. 'They're stuck tight.'

'They open electronically,' Pilbeam moaned. 'The fire must have melted the circuits.'

I grasped for inspiration. 'Clive!' I said. 'Do you think you could carry me and Shark back in through the window?'

'It's too high,' Ursula said. 'He'd need a step up . . . I know just the thing!' And she was off at a run, out of the car park.

Clive stared at me gloomily. 'I don't see what I can do,' he said, his voice mournful and slow. 'I'm just a plodding old carthorse, no use for anything except to pull a broken-down van.'

'How can you say that?' I exploded.

'You saw off Jimmy the Fridge's thugs! You saved us from the TOASTERS!'

Clive turned a melancholy eye on me. 'That was different,' he said unhappily. 'That was when I was a unicorn. Ordinary old Clive can't do those things.'

'Ordinary old Clive did do those things! That was you!'

He shook his head. 'That was Dave. Dave the fearless unicorn.'

'You were Dave!' I insisted. 'Dave was you! OK, so you thought you were a unicorn, but you were still Clive the carthorse!'

He stared blankly at me, puzzled; I continued, groping for a way to convince him. 'Clive, you don't have to be someone else. You don't have to be a unicorn, or a centaur, or Pegasus. Just be Clive; but be the best Clive you can be—not the gloomy old Clive who gives up or who runs away, but the brave, noble Clive who stands up for what's right; the Clive who doesn't give up; the Clive who is just as good as a unicorn!'

A flicker of hope flared in his eye. 'Do you really think I could?'

I reached up and touched the ring of soggy wafer, edged with tooth-marks, that still stuck to his forehead. 'I know you can. You became your best self because you thought you'd become a unicorn; but it was just you, the same Clive you've always been, with an ice-cream cone stuck to your head. It wasn't magic that turned you into a hero; it was belief in yourself. And I believe in you now, Clive. No one else can save Darcy—but you can. Will you? Will you be the hero we need?'

He stared at me, that little FLICKER now DANCING in his eye. Slowly, he raised his head up; he seemed to grow as his shoulders straightened and his chest filled with air.

'I'll try,' he said; and his voice was once more rich and resonant and filled with hope. 'I'll do my best.'

'That's all anyone can do!' I said, SCRAMBLING onto his back. 'Come on, Shark!'

I hauled her up, and Clive circled round to take a run-up. Ursula was right—the window was too high; but even as Clive got in position, I heard the ROAR of an engine, and the tow-truck came into sight, dragging Ursula's broken-down old van behind. Quickly, the polar bear positioned the van beneath the window.

'Is that about the right height?' she asked.

'I think so,' Clive said.

'Looks perfect!' I said encouragingly.

'Yay!' said Shark. 'Giddy-up, horsey!'

The horsey giddied-up. But this was not the slow and gloomy giddying-up of the old Clive; this was a fast, furious giddying-up worthy of the hero he had shown himself to be. As swiftly as an arrow he SHOT towards the window. Sure-footedly, he LEAPT. I felt the van JUDDER and QUAKE as his hooves struck it; then we were soaring through the empty frame again. Hot bitter smoke filled my lungs. I coughed; closed my eyes; felt us land.

'Whee!' said Shark, sliding off.

'Darcy?' I yelled, slipping from Clive's back.

'Here!' she called, her voice sounding choked in the heat.

'Clive!' I said. 'You can't carry all three of us. Get Darcy to safety! Shark and I will try to put the fire out.'

He nodded, and PLUNGED into the smoke.

The fire seemed to be burning most fiercely at the back of the warehouse. 'The toasters!' I said, realizing. 'One of the toasters must have started the fire when Clive kicked it back there. Quick, Shark—see if you can find something to put it out with.'

'Ice cream!' Shark exclaimed.

I almost yelled with frustration. 'This is no time for a snack!'

'What?' said Shark. 'No—I mean, we can use the ice cream to put the fire out!'

I stared at her. 'That,' I said admiringly, 'is probably the best idea you've ever had. Come on!'

I opened the nearest freezer and grabbed a tub. I could tell straight away that the ice cream had already melted. My guess was, the fire had melted the wires or fused the circuits or something, putting the freezers out of action.

As we began opening freezers and tipping liquid ice cream onto the floor, I heard hoofbeats behind me—Clive carrying Darcy to safety. We opened and tipped, opened and tipped, creating an ice-cream TSUNAMI and sending it towards the flames.

But the fire fought back, licking its way up the brickwork. By the time Clive returned for us it was clear we needed to get out, and fast.

'Quickly! Climb on my back!'

he called.

'Woooaaaaahhhh!'

he added,

sliding across the warehouse floor. 'What's this all over the floor?

Waaaaarrrgh!'

I stared, dismayed. There was an ice-cream slick covering the floor just where Clive needed to gather speed. There was no way he could leap back out through the window now. We were trapped.

Or were we?

'The van!' I yelled. 'Maybe we can use it to break down the door!'

'OK!' said Shark, and we slid as fast as we could to dryer ground and ran through the smoke towards the doors.

'Wait!' called Clive, and as I started the van he struck the doors with his hooves—once, twice, three times, kicking backwards with all his might until they started to BUCKLE.

'Out of the way, Clive!' I shouted, and
as he moved to one side I put my foot to the
floor, and we LEAPT forward. With a BANG
and a JUDDER, we hit the doors; they BURST

open and we found ourselves skidding across the car park, Clive racing after us. Smoke BILLOWED from the open doors.

'In! Quick!'
I yelled,

and Ursula and Pilbeam clambered into the van. Darcy scrambled onto Clive's back. As fast as we could, we drove to a safe distance, and there we stopped, and watched the warehouse burn.

CHAPTER SEVENTEEN

It was hard to know who was the ANGRIEST—
Pilbeam, or Ursula. They GLARED at each
other; they GLARED at Darcy and Clive; they
GLARED at me and Shark . . .

'So what am I supposed to do now?'
Pilbeam squawked. 'All my ice cream, gone
up in smoke! I'm ruined! This is your fault,
bear!'

'My fault?!'
growled Ursula.

'How is it my fault?'

'If you hadn't employed that STUPID horse, none of this would have happened!'

'And if you hadn't tried to drive me out of business, none of this would have happened!' Ursula retorted.

'And if both of you were better people, none of this would have happened!' I yelled.

That shut them up. For a moment, at least. They both turned and stared at me.

'What do you mean by that, kid?' Ursula growled.

'I mean,' I said, 'that if you two had been better bosses, things would have been very different. If Clive had been happier at work, he wouldn't have run away and got turned into a unicorn. And if Darcy's boss had had the decency to remember her name, at the very least, she might have trusted him enough to ask him for help!'

'Wait a minute,' said Pilbeam. 'Who's Darcy?'

'See?' I said. 'See? Darcy's your assistant! You're a terrible boss! And so is Ursula! So if you want to blame someone, blame yourselves!'

There was another moment of silence, during which both Ursula and Pilbeam had the grace to look slightly guilty.

'Anyway,' Pilbeam grumbled, 'how am I ever going to get my business back on track without any ice cream to sell?'

'And how am I going to sell my ice cream without a van?' Ursula muttered.

'Hang on,' I said. 'The answer's right there. What don't you work together?'

Ursula and Pilbeam stared at me in horror. 'We can't work TOGETHER!' they said together, and then turned and glared at each other.

'Why not?' I asked. 'Ursula's got ice cream

to sell; Pilbeam's got a working van to sell it from.'

'Polar bears and penguins hate each other,' Ursula said. 'It's not natural to even find us in the same place!'

'Yeah?' I said. 'Well, it's not natural for polar bears and penguins to run ice-cream businesses, either. But you manage to do it. Come to that, a lot of people would tell you it's not natural for kids to be friends with sharks—but Shark *is* my friend, and I couldn't wish for a better one. And if we can do it, so can you. So why don't you rise above your animal instincts and pool your resources?'

Ursula and Pilbeam GLARED at each other again.

'Look, it's up to you,' I said. 'You can go on hating each other and go out of business pretty darn quickly, or you can put your differences behind you, work together, and—

who knows—maybe end up running the best ice-cream business this city's ever seen.'

There was a LONG pause, and then Ursula said, 'Might work, I suppose.'

Pilbeam, not looking at anyone, muttered, 'I'll give it a go if the bear will.'

'Great,' I said. 'And if you ever have any difficulties, you'll have Darcy and Clive to help you. They're both a lot smarter than you've given them credit for.'

'Hang on!' said Ursula suddenly. 'What are we going to call the business? We may be using Pilbeam's old van, but we're not trading as Pilbeam's Ice Creams!'

'Well, we're not calling it Ursula's Ices, that's for sure!' squawked Pilbeam.

They glared at each other.

I cleared my throat meaningfully. After a moment, Ursula coughed, and said, 'Um…. Clive, what do you think?'

And Pilbeam mumbled, 'Got any ideas, Dorothy?'

There was a horrible silence, during which I thought Darcy was going to explode. And then Pilbeam looked up, realized his mistake, and said, 'I mean . . . Dur . . . Deer . . . Darcy?'

Darcy gave him a look which clearly meant, 'Don't do it again!' and looked at Clive. 'Why don't you call it Unicorn Ices?'

Ursula and Pilbeam looked at each other, and nodded. 'You know,' said Pilbeam, 'this just might work.'

CHAPTER EIGHTEEN

It was a quiet morning, a week or so later. Shark and I were having a desk-race round the office—me on Chip and Shark on Trundle, with the other desks yipping and yelping excitedly after us—when I heard a commotion in the street.

The desks rushed to the window, and Shark and I hopped down and HURRIED to the door, to see what on earth was going on.

What was going on was a huge crowd, backed up against the door to the building. I SQUEEZED forward, between the tightly pressed bodies.

The crowd was in a great mood. Clearly
something very entertaining was happening.
Ducking low, I squeezed my way to the front,
with Shark following closely behind, and
found myself staring up
at someone very
familiar.

'Child!' boomed Clive. 'And, fish!' he added, as Shark POPPED out next to me. He reared dramatically, to cheers from the crowd. In the bright daylight, the horn stuck to his forehead was clearly an ice-cream cone, but nobody seemed bothered that he wasn't a real unicorn. They were just enjoying the show.

'Yay!' said Shark. 'The horsey's being a big goat again!'

'Hey, Mark! Hi, Shark!' Darcy called, waving down from Clive's back. She slowly rose to her feet, balancing carefully as Clive turned on the spot. The crowd loved it.

'Hi, Darcy,' I said. 'What are you guys doing here?'

'We came to see you two,' a gruff voice called. I turned to see Pilbeam's ice-cream van, still a little dented and smoke-damaged from when we'd escaped the fire. Ursula and Pilbeam were leaning through the hatch, serving ice cream as quickly as they could to an **enormous** queue of snack-hungry customers. 'But first, all these people want ice cream!'

'Hurry up and scoop, bear!' Pilbeam squawked. Ursula rolled her eyes, and scooped.

It was a joy to watch them. Ursula and Pilbeam squabbled as they scooped, but not like before—now it was more like the bickering of brother and sister than the arguments of enemies. Darcy and Clive, meanwhile, clearly LOVED entertaining the crowd, and the crowd loved them.

Eventually everyone had been served and Darcy and Clive drew their tricks to a close. Their audience melted away, happily licking their ice creams.

'Looks like business is going well,' I observed.

Darcy grinned. 'It's going great.'

'Unicorn Ices is really popular!' Clive said excitedly. 'And nobody cares that I'm not a real unicorn. They like me anyway!'

'Of course they do!' Shark said. 'You're nice.' Clive tossed his mane bashfully. 'And so is the ice cream,' she added hopefully.

'It's even nicer now!' Darcy said.

Shark's eyes lit up. 'Really?' she said.

Ursula, stepping down from the van, nodded. 'Yeah,' she said. 'We sold all my ice cream in a few days, and needed to make some more. I wanted to do it my way; Pilbeam wanted to do it his way . . .'

'We had a huge row,' Pilbeam continued. 'But then Darcy reminded us that we were supposed to be working together, so we tried it.'

'It turned out that by working together, they came up with **even tastier** flavours!'

Darcy chipped in. 'And that's kind of why we're here.'

Pilbeam and Ursula GLANCED at one another, as if they weren't sure who should speak first. After a moment, Pilbeam WADDLED forward. 'We thought we owed you something,' he said. 'As a thank-you for all your help.'

'Yeah,' Ursula agreed. 'So . . . we thought we'd bring you both some ice cream.' She reached into the van, brought out a large tub, and handed it to me. I opened it up, and a DELICIOUS cool smell of raspberries hit me square in the nostrils.

'Wow!' I exclaimed. 'Thanks! If this tastes half as good as it smells, it'll be amazing!'

'And, Shark,' Pilbeam added, 'we did a bit of experimenting, and came up with something just for you.'

Darcy had climbed into the van as Pilbeam was speaking, and now she emerged again, with another large tub. She opened it up, to reveal ice cream that was smooth and grey and smelt pretty disgusting, if you asked me— kind of fishy, and kind of fatty, and definitely saltier than ice cream should ever be. Shark's eyes widened delightedly.

'Hang on,' I said. 'Is that . . . ?'

'SEAL!'

Shark yelped, and

LEAPT.

WHICH CHARACTER ARE YOU?
TAKE OUR QUIZ TO FIND OUT!

WHAT ARE YOU GOOD AT?

A) Investigating mysteries
B) Getting people out of trouble
C) Everything!
D) Spotting seals
E) Being bad

IF YOU ARE UNDER THREAT FROM A GANG OF THUGS, WHAT DO YOU DO?

A) Try and talk my way out of it
B) I'd calmly tell them off and make them go away
C) Kick them in the knees and run away magnificently
D) Imagine that they are seals and jump on them
E) No one would threaten me, I AM the thug

WHAT IS YOUR FAVOURITE GAME?

A) Cluedo
B) Monopoly
C) Musical statues. As long as there's a mirror nearby so I can admire my magnificent self
D) Find the seal
E) Murder in the dark

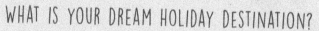

WHAT IS YOUR DREAM HOLIDAY DESTINATION?

A) Somewhere relaxing by the sea
B) An adventure holiday
C) A spa
D) Anywhere with seals
E) Somewhere exclusive and very expensive

WHAT IS YOUR GREATEST AMBITION?

A) To become a famous detective
B) To own my own business
C) To become even more magnificent, if that's even possible
D) To meet lots of seals
E) To make as much money as possible

Mostly As

You are Mark! Observant and curious, if there's a mystery then you have to get to the bottom of it!

Mostly Bs

You are Darcy! Calm and capable under pressure, if there's ever trouble everyone wants you on their side.

Mostly Cs

You are Dave the unicorn! Confident in your own magnificence, there's nothing you can't do!

Mostly Ds

You are Shark! You like seals and ... um ... it might be worth broadening your interests. Why not get a hobby?

Mostly Es

You are Jimmy the Fridge! You are ambitious and a little bit scary. You know what you want, and you're determined to get it, no matter what stands in your way.

JOHN DOUGHERTY was born in Larne, Northern Ireland. He studied psychology at university and, after a number of different jobs, became a primary school teacher. Whilst John was teaching, his interest in children's literature was reawakened and  he soon began writing stories. His books have been shortlisted for a number of prestigious awards and he was the winner of the Oscar's Book Prize, along with Laura Hughes, for the picture book *There's a Pig Up My Nose*.

KATIE ABEY is an illustrator human who lives in a teeny hobbit-like house in Derbyshire with a cat, a hedgehog, and a husband. She has illustrated lots of books including *We Wear Pants* and *We Eat Bananas*, and a number of mindfulness activity books. She has also produced work for the stationery and greeting card industries.

Ready for more great stories?
Try one of these!